The Divine Woman

BearManor Media
P.O. Box 1129
Duncan, OK 73534-1129

Phone: 580-252-3547
Fax: 814-690-1559

www.bearmanmedia.com

THE DIVINE WOMAN
by
Gladys Unger

Based on an original screenplay
by Dorothy Farnum

A Gripping Romance of Love and Pathos

Philip J Riley's

LOST FILM SERIES

BearManor Media

Candid shot of Greta Garbo with Lowell Sherman during the shooting of the film.

The Divine Woman

INTRODUCTION
BY
PHILIP J. RILEY

The Divine Woman is considered a "Lost Film" Only a short nine minute sequence with Russian subtitles has survived, discovered in 1993 at the Gosfilmofond, Moscow.

My interest in "Lost Films" started while I was working for Forrest J Ackerman, at the Ackerman Archives.

While researching my first "Lost Film" book, Lon Chaney's, MGM production #330, *London After Midnight* from 1927, I discovered that *The Divine Woman* had been stored only 2 productions away, in the same MGM vault where a fire destroyed everything in the mid- 1960s.

Adapted from the 1925 play Starlight by Gladys Unger which starred Doris Keane, the plot is loosely based on stories of the early life of the French actress Sarah Bernhardt. Marianne (Greta Garbo) is a poor French girl who goes to Paris in the 1860s to seek her fortune as an actress. As she rises to success in the theatre, she must choose between the romantic attentions of two men: Lucien (Lars Hanson), a passionate young army deserter who goes to jail after stealing a dress for her, and Henry Legrand (Lowell Sherman), a Paris producer who offers her fame and fortune.

Directed by Victor Sjöström
Produced by Richard A. Rowland
John Colton (titles)
Dorothy Farnum (screenplay)
Gladys Unger (play *Starlight*)
Starring Greta Garbo

Gladys Unger

Cinematography Oliver T. Marsh
Editing by Conrad A. Nervig
Distributed by MGM
Release date January 14, 1928
Running time 80 minutes
Budget $266,817.14

Greta Garbo as Marianne - Marah in the 1st draft
Lars Hanson as Lucien
Lowell Sherman as Henry Legrand -(Carre)
Polly Moran as Mme. Pigonier
Dorothy Cumming as Mme. Zizi Rouck, Marianne's
Mother - (Rosine)
Johnny Mack Brown as Jean Lery
Cesare Gravina
Paulette Duval as Paulette
Jean De Briac as Stage Director

It is my hope to reconstruct this film using photographs, set stills and silent film titles as I did with *London After Midnight*. But until the film is "found" I hope this novel, based on the final shooting script, provides a glimpse of what the film was like.

Please note that this novelette was based on the first shooting script and like *London After Midnight*, it went through editorial changes before it was aproved by Irving Thalberg and reached the screen.

Philip J Riley
December 2011
Information gathered from MGM Central Files and www.wikipedia.org/

CHAPTER I

A Precious Pearl

THE early morning calm of a quiet street in Paris was rudely shattered by the ringing steps of a man hurrying with long swinging strides that bespoke a desperate haste. Sleep hung in the drowsy spring air, for this was the Montmarte section of Paris where "day" starts at sundown and the feverish, pleasure-craving activities of this scintillating quarter only end with the first peep of dawn over the house tops. So Montmarte was asleep and only an occasional charwoman took note of the hurrying figure.

Monsieur Antoine Carre rushed across a bright courtyard without pause and halted abruptly at the portal of an imposing house. He was a man of about forty, the richness of whose apparel proclaimed him one of means. To the keen observer, some touch of extreme fashion in his clothes indicated his vocation as other than that of the successful business or professional man. He was the type usually associated with the theatre and, true to type, Carre was the successful owner of the famed Theatre Carre, where Parisians had learned to expect a brilliancy of production and an artistic excellence second to no other stage in the gay French capitol.

Some women would have called him handsome, but certain hard lines around the mouth and a cold, steely glitter in the eyes gave a hint of worldly cynicism and dire cruelty that marred one's first favorable impression of the man.

Carre rang the door bell furiously. To impatient to await the answer to this summons, he rapped violently on the door with his cane. Carre was out of sorts and in a nasty temper at being roused from his slumbers at so early an hour. He was at a loss to guess the reason for the urgency of the message sent him by Rosine, fair occupant of this house; provoked at Rosine for being so unreasonable as to send for him at so unearthly an hour; piqued at her perversity in keeping the reason for her summons a secret and, perhaps, a little worried too.

Again he started a violent tattoo with his cane on the panels of the door, at the same time keeping his finger on the bell-button.

A startled lackey, answering this wild clamor, barely escaped a blow from the pounding cane as he opened the door. Carre unceremoniously pushed past the servant, thrusting his hat, cane and gloves into the astonished man's hands as he rushed toward the staircase.

The Divine Woman

There was a strange air of solemn gloom pervading the house that Carre, in his haste, failed to notice. Neither did he give a second glance to a weeping lady's maid passing him upon the stairs, nor to a group of other household servants talking in low awed tones.

Carre mounted the stairs two at a time, arriving in the hall above just as a nurse, in her spic-and-span white costume, tiptoed from a nearby room.

"What is it?" asked Carre breathlessly of the quiet efficient woman.

"Madame is dying!"

"Dying?" gasped Carre, taken aback. "Oh," in a relieved tone, "is that all? I thought it was something really important. But if Madame is merely dying again, perhaps I can be of assistance."

Carre brushed past the astonished nurse, who shook her head in silent wonderment at such flippant talk at such a solemn time. He knocked softly, and without waiting for an answer, opened the door to a luxuriantly furnished boudoir.

In a great, elaborate canopied bed in the very center of the big room, Madame lay half hidden among beautiful silken spreads and great downy pillows. At least Madame would die in comfort.

Rosine, for so was Madame known to her friends, was a dainty creature whose cold beauty was beginning to fade. Yet there was still much of attractiveness remaining to the soft, regular features, the deep blue eyes and the brilliant blond head, and Rosine had taken pains to see that none of her beauty should be lost even upon so tragic an occasion as her death.

Rosine the pampered, the center around which gyrated one of the many wild circles of the Paris latin quarter, was pentulant, quick-tempered and insincere. A creature of whims, her latest prank, perhaps suggested by a headache from the gay party of the night before, was to thus announce her untimely demise.

She peeped at her visitor between tapering fingers, hands pressed to her suffering brow. When she recognized Carre, the blue eyes fluttered, closed, and her pose, as near as she could make it, was one of great suffering.

Carre crossed to the bed with jaunty step, a cynical smile twisting his lips. His manner was that of one entering a drawing room and, in the ordinary tone of one greeting a friend he said:

"Good morning, my dear Rosine, they tell me you are dying. It is good to know that you thought of me at a time like this.

He lifted her hand and with mock ceremony kissed it, then, with ironic carefulness, placed it gently back upon the pain-wracked brow. He stood for a moment amusedly looking down upon the figure before him and with a sarcasm he did not attempt to hide he said:

"I am sorry, Rosine, you are so near the end of life's happy span. I'm sure life has been happy for you and you part from it with regret. The last time you died, so they say, you wanted rubies. What is it you want now?

Rosine, smarting from Carre's taunt, forgot her pose and sat bolt upright in bed. Her quick temper-mastered her and she abandoned herself to an uncontrollable paroxysm of anger that verged upon hysterics. As Carre stood silently and smilingly watching her, she presently quieted and, pressing her hands to her eyes from which she managed to squeeze a few tears, she answered Carre's last remark in a voice of injured feelings:

"How can you talk to me so, Carre, when you see how ghastly ill I am? I thought truly I was dying when I sent for you, expecting so dear a friend to console me. Instead you flout me. What do I want, my dear Carre?—I want nothing but your friendship."

Carre bowed profoundly, and with the cynical smile again playing around his lips, he answered:

"Madame honors me" and then laughing he continued, "what a great actress you would make, Rosine, have you ever thought of putting yourself under my management? The Theatre Carre would ring with applause for such superb acting, as I now applaud," and Carre clapped politely as Rosine stared at him furiously.

Again the woman's anger got the better of her and she tore at the coverlet, flung the pillows about the bed and hugged her knees as she writhed under the open scorn of her visitor. In a voice of one unjustly criticized she said.

"Of all the people who have gathered here at my home so often, not once has been a real friend. I know that, but I thought that you, Carre, were different."

In a woebegone voice she continued: "No man has ever understood me," and with a deep sigh paused. Then brightening, she exclaimed: "Ah yes! I am wrong.

There was one. One who loved and understood me, my dearly beloved husband."

Carre raised his eyebrows and smiled ironically as he teased:

"And what did he give you?—pearls?"

Rosine flew into another fury and blurted out defensively: "Yes, that is what he gave me. A pearl, a single, priceless pearl; a dear little child to love and cherish. Taunt me as you will, Carre; laugh at me; scorn me, but I have a treasure beyond price—my priceless pearl!" and she fell to musing, with an expression in her cold eyes as close to mother-love as this hard, pleasure-loving and worldly-wise woman could ever approach.

Carre for the first time showed evidences of a lively interest. He had known Rosine for several years, joining in the gaety of her many parties; mixing with the group of artists, writers and the usual number of artistic pretenders of the latin quarter who made Rosine's house a rendezvous. He had long wondered at the mystery of Rosine's past and by adroit questioning had often sought to solve the riddle. But Rosine had always been too deft for him, parrying his questions without revealing her secret. Now here was a revelation, and Carre sought to follow up the clue.

"Ah, a child," he exclaimed. "A precious pearl. You must, of course, be proud of the little dear, but where is it?"

Rosine bit her lips. She had not meant to reveal the secret and was furiously angry at being so indiscreet. She vented her fury as before by throwing the pillows around and tearing the coverlet of the bed.

Carre smiled at her childish display of temper and continued his questioning. "Tell me, dear Rosine, how big is this pearl of yours and where have you hidden it?"

But Rosine interrupted him angrily: "Do stop pestering me, Carre. What business is it of yours where the child is or even that I have one. I live in the present, the past is forgotten, so why do you bring up sad memories," and she tried hard to cry for the possible effect it might have upon her inquisitor. But the habit of years of having but one purpose in life, her own selfish interests, had moulded this woman into a cast of ice which no warmth of human emotions could melt, and Rosine found it difficult to attain the proper pose to go with her claim of softening sad memories.

Carre saw through her acting and continued his questioning relentlessly:

"But at least Rosine, you can tell me the child's name and its whereabouts. I don't want to bring back sad memories, as you call them, but since you, yourself, started this flow of confidences why not go the whole way and tell me all?"

Rosine flung herelf back upon the pillows petulantly. She recognized that the easiest way out for her was to tell Carre what he wanted to know, so she answered:

"Well, if you must know, the child is about eighteen. She is called Marah. I have not seen her in years. I felt that Paris and this house was not the place for a growing girl, so I have placed her on a farm in Anvergne where she is far happier than if she made her home with me" With this self justification of her actions, Rosine relaxed and presently continued:

"And now Carre, you need not question me further. I have told you what you asked and if you continue to pry into my private affairs I shall merely stuff my ears."

But Carre had learned what he wanted to know and a sardonic grin played upon his features as he revolved in his mind a wicked plan. He prepared to leave, lifting Rosine's hand to his lips with an elaborate show of respect as he said:

"I shall not bother you about the pearl any more, Rosine. Forgive me for having disturbed you. I hope you quickly recover; I bid you adieu."

Rosine raised herself upon an elbow as Carre started to elave and as he finished she quickly spoke:

"Adieu my friend. Pardon my show of temper, but you must know I am really ill. Now promise me you will come to my birthday party."

Carre promised briefly to be present and hurried away. He had no time to lose if he was to put into effect the plan which had suggested itself when Rosine revealed her secret.

Rosine's parties were famous in Montmarte. Anything and everything served as an excuse for her to give one, and many and often were her "birthday" parties. Her guests conveniently forgot that perhaps but a few months before they had attended another of Rosine's birthday celebrations and never troubled to remind Rosine that her birthday came with unwonted frequency.

No expense or pains were spared at these festivities and many were the novel effects that Rosine accomplished. She had lavished unusual attention on this, her latest "birthday" party.

On a marble terrace of her beautiful home; under the spreading branches of trees that reached from the court below; softly lighted be festooned silken-shaded lanterns, Rosine's guests are found seated at the round table with its snowy linen and beautiful floral decorations. The rich service, the shining silverware and glittering glasses, and the sparkling jewels of the handsomely-gowned ladies all combine to create such a scene of spendor and magnificence as have made Rosine's dinner the talk of Montmarte.

The dinner started on a note of discreet gaiety. Congratulations on Rosine's birthday were laughinglymade and the presents opened and admired. Of the twenty places around the festive board only one was vacant

The chair at Rosine's right right, intended for Carre, was empty. Rosine pouted. Had Carre forgotten? Perhaps, or even more likely, he had deliberately stayed away to fout her. Rosine's temper, ever short, mounted with the passing moments. Her partner on the left, and elderly man with grey hair and a face showing the deep set marks of heavy dissipation, leaned toward her. He was jealout of Carre's monopoly of Rosine's interest and seized the opportunity for thrusting in a few shafts of sarcasm. Adjusting his monocle with great deliberation, and with an effected tone of deep solicitude, he said softly to Rosine:

"I hope our friend Carre has not had an accident. Nothing, I know, could keep him away from one of your parties except ill fate and we all share your worries." As Rosine's only reply was a set, forced smile, he continued:

"By the way, have you seen Carre's latest 'find'? She is a beauty and I am told that the Theatre Carre will soon have another . . . . ," but he got no further. Rosine interrupted him rudely with: "Please—I have a headache; I'd rather not talk."

As Rosine finished speaking she raised her eyes toward the entrance, to ther behold Carre making his belated arrival. A gleam came to the cold blue eyes and her mouth set in a grim line as she prepared to receive her tardy guest.

Carre entered casually, as though unaware of his lateness, and in his usual nonchalant manner sauntered toward the table. He greeted each guest with some laughing remark as he passed until finally he stood bending toward the unsmiling face of his hostess.

"Well, here I am Rosine; you see I have not forgotten."

He reached down to raise her hand to his lips, but she snatched it pentulantly away as she answered him in low angry tone:

"You are late; you have kept us all waiting and you have no apology for your rudeness. No, you have not forgotten the dinner, for that means food, but you have forgotten something else. My birthday"—and with tears in her voice—"my birthday and you forgot . . . ."

"Madame," said Carre in injured tones, "how could you ever thing I should forget the day that ushered into the world the most beautiful, the most . . . ."

but he left off with a laugh, not bothering to finish the flamboyant and obviously insincere compliment he started.

All the guests had stopped talking; all were listening and watching the two. Rosine pretended not to notice the flippant manner of Carre's speech; in fact, she had but one idea, and her greedy hand went out in response to that idea.

"You haven't forgotten?" in a guestioning tone which she tried to make coquettish, "then the dear boy is forgiven. But if you haven't forgotten where is it; where is my present?"

Carre smiled his ironic smile. "Madame in impatient. With your permission I must ask you to come into the house, where you will find your present. If Madame will be so kind," and he offered his arm.

Rosine arose with alacrity. "In the house," she purred, "what can it be." Then turning back to her guests as she passed toward the door with Carre she said:

"Dear friends, please excuse me. Continue with your dinner, don't wait for us. Laugh, laugh—be gay," and she flung up her arms with a little cry, then hurried away with Carre.

There was a general buzz of excited comment among Rosine's guests as the latter passed beyond hearing. Rosine and her doings were a never-ending source of gossip within the circle of those who frequented her perpetual dinners and parties. Rosine liked to talk of her "salon" where were gathered the wit and genius of Paris' Latin quarter, and it must be said that she attracted to her small circle a number who had made marked successes in writing, music and the drama.

The banquet proceeded, while Rosine impatiently hurried with Carre for a peep at his mysterious present. Through a great marble hall Carre led her to the drawn portieres of the drawing room. He drew near on tip-toe, with a great display of mystery, enjoining silence on Rosine by placing his finger on his lips.

Slowly he drew aside the heavy portieres and motioned Rosine to look. A strange scene met her gaze and she glanced at Carre with a questioning look. At his nod toward the room she again turned her attention to the scene before her.

A stranger had invaded Rosine's handsome drawing room. A young girl dressed in the quaint but clumsy costume of the Province of Anvergne was moving as lightly as a humming bird from one lovely thing to another.

She seemed to take infinite pleasure in merely touching with the ends of her fingers each object as she came to it. As gently as the touch of a soft summer's breeze she placed the very tips of her fingers on an exquisite vase; she rubbed her hand ever so lightly along the back of a beautiful gilded chair and then stopped and placed her finger tips on the rich brocaded upholstery. Suddenly she dropped to her hands and knees and brushed her palms across the soft nap of the rich oriental rug. She arose and moved to a window where she smoothed a silken curtain; again in the middle of the room she arose on tip-toe to touch the glittering crystals of a magnificent chandelier. She walked slowly toward a great mirror reaching from floor to ceiling where she stood for a long moment looking at her relection, the reflection of a pretty girl with eyes big with wonder and delight.

For a second or two she made quick birdlike motions with her hands to various parts of her costume, tucking in a plait here, smoothing a wrinkle there. And unfamiliar object near the mirror then claimed her attention and she bent to examine more closely an exquisitely made antique music box. Its use was a closed book to her and she inspected it curiously. She moved a lever by accident and was startled when the mechanism whirred and a dainty tinkle of music followed.

The girl stood up, delighted with the music and wrapped in wonder. Presently the spell of the lively tune enticed her and, seizing a beautiful Spanish shawl nearby, she draped it becomingly about her slender, shapely body, and in a moment was in the whirl of an exotic dance.

The lilt and gaiety of the music; the breath of flowers; the graceful sweep of birds in flight; the joy of just being alive—all these the girl naively portrayed in her quaint little fold dance.

Forward and backward she moved in time with the music; then a dizzy pirouette half-way across the room and back. Light as a leaf gently wafted by the breeze she danced, coquetting with an imaginary partner. Then, with bubbling merriment, her movements became quicker, till she reached a wild dance of utter abandonment. Sensing that the music was nearing its close, the girl changed her steps so that in its final stages her dance became a symphony of joyous movement; an animated picture of ineffable grace and charm. As the music stopped the girl whirled on her toes, her skirts switching with her rapid motion, and with eyes sparkling she made a graceful courtesy toward the music box. The entire spontaneous performance had been a rare exhibition; no stage ever showed a more entrancing spectacle. The girl and her dance had been enchanting, and now, as she finished her courtesy, with flushed cheeks and flashing eyes, the charm of her impromtu performance seemed to cling to her like the delicate odor of some rare perfume. She carefully placed the gorgeous shawl back upon the table from which she had taken it, lingering in the action as though loath to part with the beautiful fabric. She turned to resume her delightful exploring among the treasures of the exquisite room, when she was started by a sound from the doorway.

Rosine, with Carre beside her, had watched the charming dance. Rosine looked on with mixed feelings of resentment at the intrusion of this peasant girl and a gruding admiration for the excellence of the girl's dancing. Carre had watched breathlessly, enthralled by the girl's charm and the quality of her performance; his knowledge of the theatre making it evident to him that the girl possessed a natural talent.

As the dance stopped, Rosine, released from the spell which held her motionless in spite of herself, now swept haughtily into the room, followed by the smiling Carre, who appeared amused by the situation. Rosine approached the intruder with a menacing gesture and her furious questions came in a hoarse, striden tone:

"Who are you? What do you mean by coming here, snooping among my personal belongings, using my drawing room for a disgusting peasant dane. How dare you?"

Rosine paused, out of breath and at a loss to find adequate words to express her indignation. But this snip of a girl faced her unafraid; instead of cowering from her as Rosine had expected, the stranger actually burst out laughing.

What could it mean. Astonished, Rosine looked to Carre with a question in her eyes. Recovering a little, she managed to stammer.

"Carre, what is this. I believe you are behind it all. Who is she?"

Rosine was angry, so angry that she trembled and could hardly form the question. Her voice was pitched high and shrill and Carre, to quiet her, patted her arm reassuringly and in a quiet, soothing voice said:

"Calm yourself Rosine. There's nothing to get so excited about."

Then, pausing for dramatic effect and placing one arm around the waist of the young girl and the other across the shoulder of the still angry woman, he drew the two closer together and said in a portentous manner:

"Let me introduce the little stranger to you Rosine." He stopped and then resumed and in a tone of formal presentation:

"The pearl; the precious pearl."

The girl was still laughing, in the same manner

which had so shocked Rosine, and at the climax of Carre's strange introduction she still chuckled in glee.

Carre had told the girl that he was taking her to the home of her mother, and when he left her alone in the drawing room he had assured her that he would bring her mother to this room. When Rosine became so angry, pouring out her resentment at the intrusion, the girl had considered it a great joke that her mother did not know her and treated her as a stranger.

As Carre completed his introduction, Rosine drew back quickly and gasped. She was stunned, to surprised and startled to speak for the moment. She stared at the girl, hostility seeming to radiate from her. Her cold blue eyes took on a gleam of ice light; the mouth became set into a hard straight line; and angry frown darkened the fair brow. She was the personification of hate as she hissed:

"Marah—you—here!"

The girl, or Marah, as we now know her, seemed not to notice the cold, distant, even hostile attitude of the woman she had been looking forward to meeting with such delight. Here before her was her mother— "mother," how nice it seemed just to think the word. Her mother, whom she had longed to be with for so many years; her mother whom she had never seen to remember; her mother, whom she had adored with almost a religious fevor. Here, within arms reach was the one she had so desired; here was the moment for which all her life she had been waiting and longing.

With tears streaming from her eyes, with an expression of utter joy and happiness, Marah held forth her arms with a glad cry of pent-up-longing:

"Mother."

But Rosine drew back, the cold scorn still in her manner, the dark frown still clouding her face. Her thoughts raced: this creature, her daughter; this strange person with silly costume, the heavy, clumsy shoes, this rude peasant—her daughter!

But Marah failed even now to notice anything amiss in the way she was received. Perhaps this was the way mothers usually acted, especially beautiful and rich mothers; she could not tell, for she had never before had any experience with a mother of her own. Marah drew to Rosine's side reverently. She made a half motion as though to touch this radiant woman she could hardly believe was her mother. She was too overcome with joy at the long dreamed-of meeting, too over-whelmed with wonder at her mother's beauty to speak, but presently she overcame her timidity sufficiently to cry in a low trembling voice:

"Mother, I have dreamed of you, longed for you, wanted you so badly. How happy I am to find you. I used to think you would be like the Madonna at the way-side shrine, only you are more beautiful."

As the girl started to speak, Rosine's resentment changed to amazement. Rosine had an accurate esti-mate of her own worth; she well knew the uselessness of her wasted life of selfishness and pleasure; her entire lack of any redeeming trait. To have this girl compare her to a Madonna struck her with surprise, then embar-rassment. And when Marah spoke of her beauty her vanity responded to the compliment. The hard lines of her face relaxed and she smiled. Marah, encouraged by the smile, rushed to her, and flinging her arms about her, held Rosine fast.

Clinging closely to her mother, her hungry heart overflowing with joy to be in her mother's arms, Marah shed tears of happiness. Tenderly she whispered"

"I am so happy, darling mother, so happy that I'm sad. That's why I am crying now. To be here in this beautiful place with you is like going to Heaven without dying."

Rosine was bewildered; she had no answer ready for the young girl who held her so tightly in her strong arms. The palpitating form warm against her own body; the low intense tone; the great joy in the fair face upturned to hers combined to bring back memories that Rosine thought were buried for all time deep in her past. Some feeble, dim spark of motherlove, hidden within her, was touched. The reserve of manner which still persisted and the last vestige of coldness in the face began to fade entirely and words of endearment—sincere words such as Rosine had not uttered in years—trembled on her lips. Instinctively she made a motion as though to press Marah to her, but as she raised her head her glance happened to fall on Carre.

An evil grin spread over Carre's face. He had thoroughly enjoyed the little drama he had so skillfully arranged and now, as he sensed the climax approaching, for he read the changing thoughts that swept across Rosine's features, he prepared to witness the miracle of this cold, distant, selfish woman of the world, changing to at least some semblance of a kind, loving mother.

It would indeed be a miracle and one wrought by him, but he took no pride in what might be a worthy deed. Instead he had a devilish delight in his work, for he knew that Marah, acknowledged as Rosine's daughter, would mean many difficult and embarrassing complcations for the latter.

Rosine read his thoughts in that fleeting glimpse and instantly her manner changed, her figure stiffened and the hard, cruel lines reappeared in her face.

She hated Carre for the rude joke he has played upon her; she detested this crude peasant girl, and violently, angrily she pushed the surprised Marah from her.

The lace of Rosine's handsome gown, entangled in a button of Marah's costume, gave with a low rending sound as Marah staggered backward. This small damage, trifling at most, seemed to fan the almost insane fury of the woman.

"Get away from me you crude, awkward beast," she hissed at the cowering girl and then, turning to Carre, she tore at him like a tigeress. Carre, the devil, was to blame for this and the overflowing caldron of her boiling anger poured out upon him.

"How dare you, Carre! How dare you play such a joke on me? I could tear your eyes out; I hate you." The words snapped and sputtered from her like the spitting electric sparks from the bare ends of a live wire. She became incoherent for a space and then in a fierce whisper she continued:

"You know I can't have that here," with a contemptuous nod toward the weeping Marah. "Do you want

want to spoil my salon with that crude peasant?" She stamped her foot and her voice rose to a scream:

"Get her away from here before I am disgraced."

Marah, too surprised at first to realize what her mother's sudden action meant, awoke at last to the cruel import of the words. Was she to be forsaken? She waited breathlessly as the angry woman stormed at the still smiling Carre.

With Rosine's last words, Marah no longer had room to doubt. What sort of a mother had she found?—something to despise, and passionately she cried:

"Pig woman."

Rosine stared at the scornful girl. The loathing in Marah's voice and the contempt written upon the girl's face disconcerted the woman, and she yielded a step or two backward as the flushed girl drew near her. Carre was thrilled by the scene before him as he had never before been thrilled by the greatest drama played upon the stage of his theatre. He prepared to enjoy himself.

Marah went close to her mother, her face thrust forward till it was but inches from the surprised, and shocked, and somewhat alarmed features of Rosine. In a tone wherein hate and loathing strove for mastery, the girl spoke:

"Pig woman—that is what we honest country folk call women who abandon their children in the fields for the pigs to find."

Marah spat upon the floor before her mother; the supreme gesture of contempt in the code of the peasant.

Rosine waited for no more. She turned and ignominously fled from the wrath of the girl. Carre had watched, no detail of the scene escaping him, and he now glanced irresolutely from Marah who had collapsed upon a chair with her face buried in her hands, to Rosine who almost ran toward the terrace and her waiting guests.

He paused for a moment to reassure the weeping girl saying: "Stay here in this room till I return. I will be back in a moment."

"Do you understand—" he asked, bending over the girl and upon her nod he hurried after Rosine.

As Rosine reached the banquet scene she tried to compose herself, but her torn dress and distraught manner which she could not conceal revealed to her guests that something unusual had happened. They watched her as she swept to her place at the table, all silent, waiting for her words of explanation, but Rosine failed to satisfy their curiosity.

As she seated herself the elderly gentleman at her left, who had before annoyed her with his remarks about Carre's lateness in arriving, seized upon this occasion to continue his attack.

"But pardon, Madame," he said in a purring tone, "may I ask what present friend Carre brought you?"

Rosine was embarrassed and bit her lips nervously as she strove to find a plausible answer. A brilliant thought flashed to her and she answered with a laugh?

"Carre's present?—a most lovely one—a portrait of my dear departed husband."

With her laughing answer the tension was relaxed and Rosine with her friends entered into the spirit of the banquet, as though no untoward incident had occurred to spoil even for a brief space the gaiety of the evening.

CHAPTER II

"LUCIEN"

Carre at first had hurried after Rosine and had reached the entrance to the terrace just in time to hear her describe his "present."

He hesitated to rejoin the party. Here was a scene long familiar to him, something he could have any night he sought it. But back in the drawing room was something not to be had so easily. He withdrew from the entrance hastily and hurried back through the hall.

He paused at the doorway to gaze at the girl who, now that he had time to study her closely, he grudgingly admitted to himself was beautiful. She had her mother's deep blue eyes, but softened with a light that made them deep pools of moon-lit water. The small oval of her face was framed by a mass of waving chestnut hair that in a slant of light showed glints of dull gold. Long lashes under the curving beauty of daintily-arched brows; full lips that disappeared in soft curves which promised a disposition perverse and mischievous, and somtimes wistful, completed a picture that Carre was not slow to appreciate.

Marah was weeping bitterly, disgusted with herself for caring so much. Carre went to her softly and stooped to soothe the sobbing girl. Under the guise of sympathy he caressed her. He looked at her admiringly as he spoke the words that so often had left his lips when in the presence of hysterical women:

"What an actress you would make."

The girl started. "Actress" she exclaimed, "you say actress when my heart is breaking." A second later another thought came and she smiled through her tears as she said: "I've always wanted to be an actress. I used to watch the strolling players when they came at fair time."

Carre looked bored. Just another stage-struck girl like so many he knew. But, after all, he thought, she was not so like the silly, scatter-brain type who pestered him to give them a chance in his theatre. She was different somehow and he looked at her appraisingly.

"There is no reason why you can't be an actress," he assured her confidentially. "It will be very simple to make you one. I am Carre, of the Theatre Carre."

He spoke as though his word alone was enough to make her great and, although Marah had never heard of the Theatre Carre, she was quick enough to grasp that this man had it within his power to help her in her secret ambition. Marah was enraptured and her recent sorrow was forgotten as she listened hungrily to Carre's words.

"It is all very easy and simple, little Marah. I have my own theatre which is one of the most popular and successful in Paris. Under my guidance and direction I can make you a wonderful actress in a very short time and, alors!—here is your first lesson."

Marah had hung upon his words and half in a daze at the brilliant prospect opened before her, she was unresisting as Carre caught her in a passionate embrace. But the girl realized her position in an instant and fought fiercely against him, pushing Carre from her before he could touch her lips.

Carre's vanity was wounded and he spoke testily as he adjusted his tie:

"You, the daughter of the pig woman, and you take offense over a little thing like that."

Marah's eyes blazed. She might call her mother that—with enough justification too—but never would she allow anyone else to insult even so cruel a mother. In a tempest of indignation she seized the first thing to her hand, and viciously beat Carre about the head with a heavy book from the table. Carre stumbled backward, the attack coming so quickly and unexpectedly that he could but ineffectively ward off the blows of the sturdy girl, whose natural strength, resulting from her country life was made even greater by her anger. He tripped over a chair and fell heavily backward, his head striking the sharp edge of a stool.

He lay unconscious, a crumpled heap upon the floor, and as the girl stared down at him appalled, her heart failed her. She knelt at his side, but to her started eyes there was no sign of life. The small tirckle of blood where his head had struck was enough to complete her terror and she scrambled to her feet, wild-eyed, with but one thought—escape!

Marah ran from the room, down the long hall toward a door-way that promised freedom. But reaching what she supposed a haven, she found it far otherwise, for she stood upon the entrance to the terrace where the uproarious party was in progress.

The frightened girl hurried back along the hall seeking another exit. A servant appeared upon the stairs at the other end of the hall, cutting off Marah's escape there, so the flustered girl re-entered the drawing room, circled as far as she could around the still figure on the floor and with one last, hasty and fearful glance at the huddled heap in the center of the room, Marah wtenched open a window and leaped lightly to the ground a few feet below.

The servant, suspicious of the stranger and noticing the great haste of the girl, had followed her to the drawing room. He quickly revived Carre and then hastened to the window prepared to give the alarm, but Carre motioned for him to stop and dismissed the man with a nod of thanks.

Meanwhile, Marah, with fear clutching her heart, hurried through the dark streets, trying ever to keep within the deeper gloom at the side of the houses, starting breathless at every sound, and frightened ever and anon by the play of moonlight on the pavement before her. Crouching in door-ways to avoid passers-by, scurrying across intersecting streets like a frightened rabbit, Marah hurried on, hopelessly lost, not knowing or caring where she went just so she could put the greatest possible distance between her and the scene of her supposed crime.From a cross street unexpectedly the sound of men singing reached her. Lustily voices, in a not untuneful chorus, were singing uproariously a quaint old soldier's song:

"When I was a musketeer
A—ron—ron—ron
Petet—pat—pon!
Of the gayest regiment!"

Marah slipped into the shadow of a door-way hoping that the singers would continue on without turning down the street. But her hopes were vain, for the gay group wheeled to the left at the crossing with many a tipsy lurch and stumble and came directly toward the frightened girl.

She flattened herself in the shallow space, trying to make herself as small as possible, but to no avail. A soldier spied her, paused in front of her and bending forward, hands on knees, made himself heard above the din of singing.

"Comrades, look! What have we here? A little bird, lost from her nest," and he laughed uproariously at what he considered a clever witicism.

The singing stopped and the group of boisterous soldiers crowded toward the door-way to stare at the cringing girl. Many were the ribald comments and one, more venturesome than the rest, grasped Marah by the arm and drew her out into the street. There, under the light of a blinking street lamp, a dozen or more of the men formed a ring around the still frightened girl, holding her captive while their comrades stood along the sidewalk watching the fun. They danced around her, teasing and tormenting her. Each time she made a dash at a gap in the circle around her, the men closed in, forcing her again to the center of the group although Marah fought them like a wild creature.

Here was great fun; see the pretty little devil fight; the soldiers in their drunken prank took great delight in annoying the pretty girl. But in spite of their brute strength the girl, fighting desperately, more than held her own. She pulled off the cap of one, yanking his hair till he called out for mercy; she pulled the nose of another, the while he called to his comrades for assistance. The men watching from the side-walk enjoyed the fun, calling encouragement to the girl and laughing at the discomforture of Marah's victims. Finally, Marah dodged under the arms of the encircling men and made a dash for liberty. In her blind flight she ran full tilt into the arms of a soldier who had all the while stood somewhat apart, seemingly not altogether approving of his comrades' antics, but still smiling at the scene.

The soldier seized Marah's hands, remembering the damage she had wrought with them but a moment before, and holding her fast he gazed full into her face.

"Bon, but she is pretty," he muttered and Marah, seeing in him just another tormentor, by a supreme effort wrenched herself free and fled down the street.

The men, tired of their amusement and due shortly at their barracks, did not pursue the flying girl, but continued on their way, singing the gay soldier song, so oddly interrupted not long before.

The soldier with whom Marah had collided in her flight stared first at the figure of the girl running up the street and then at his comrades, now resuming their tumultuous progress to the barracks.

If he followed the girl it would mean over-staying his leave, with punishment swift and sure. He took a hesitating step toward his departing comrades, a second step, slower than the first, and then, throwing caution and sense of duty to the winds, he turned resolutely down the street where he still could see the form of the girl who, realizing the men had not followed her, had now slowed down to a weary trot. Those blue eyes and that pretty face had decided him and with a swift stride he followed after the girl.

Marah, weary with her headlong flight and her encounter with the soldiers, continued with lagging steps She reached the famous old Moulin de la Gallette, celebrated through all of Paris as a lover's lane. Wearily she started up the well-worn steps, flanked by great clusters of white lilacs showing an eerie brilliancy of startling beauty as seen in the changing light of the bright moonlight.

It was the ideal setting for romance, but romance was far from Marah's thoughts as she paused to rest. Only for a second did she stop, for a step behind her claimed her attention and the hated soldier's uniform was enough to set her again in full flight. But the girl's dash this time was short. Half-way up the steps she tripped; the stiff starched petticoat of her picturesque peasant costume, loosened in her wild run, sagged around her knees and finally became hopelessly entangled around her feet, bringing the panting girl to a stop.

The soldier caught up with her and Marah, handicapped as she was, prepared to give battle. She recognized the soldier who had held her for a moment when she broke from the ring of her tormentors. Somehow she did not dislike this one so much as she did those who had held her captive, for she had had a glimpse of a pleasant face with laughing eyes and she instinctively knew, even in that fleeting moment, that she could trust him. But she was furious that he should catch her in so embarrassing a position and it was a flushed, angry face she turned to him as she clutched her trailing petticoat.

The soldier did not try to conceal his merriment over her predicament and he doubled over with laughter as he watched her. Finally he managed to ask in a teasing tone:

"Why are you running away; have you stolen something? What is that you are holding; is that the loot?"

Marah disregarded his little joke, but she could not overlook the suggestion that she had stolen something. To steal was the worst sin in her catagory, so letting go her petticoat, she raised her hand to solemnly sweat her innocence.

Then she remembered the embarrassing garment and in a panic reached to clutch the fallen petticoat. The soldier was enjoying himself tremendously and, still laughing, in a teasing tone he pressed her:

"Then if you did not steal, why were you running? Tell me, perhaps I can help you."

Marah looked at him searchingly and decided she could confide in him, so in a breathless voice she answered:

"I think I killed a man."

The soldier retreated a step in alarm, but stopped to stare at her incredulously. She stood plaintive and sad, so he returned to her side and asked:

"But why?"

A bitter memory flashed through Marah's mind and she answered sullenly:

"Because he tried to kiss me."

The soldier stared at her, stunned by her utter simplicity. After a moment's thought he decided that this girl, fight though she might with fists and nails, could not have killed a man; the very idea made him laugh. Marah watched the changing thoughts of the man, reflected in his open countenance. She looked up at him pleadingly like a hurt and sensitive child and the soldier drew very close as he whispered:

"You will soon have to kill me."

Marah at first failed to grasp his meaning, forgetting for the moment that she had said she killed a man because he tried to kiss her. Then, realizing the signigicance of the soldier's remark, she tossed her head saucily as though to say that he had better not try to kiss her or he would fare no better than the other.

The soldier, watching her closely, made up his mind that discretion was the better part of valor with this fiery little creature, and changed his tactics.

With a fine flourish he presented himself, saluting her soldier-wise as he said:

"Allow me to introduce myself. At your service, mademoiselle—Lucien Andriot—soldier of France!"

He was very proud of being a soldier of France and Marah was greatly impressed by his importance. She curtsied peasant fashion saying: "My name is Marah."

"Marah," Lucien said softly, "what a pretty name. It's late, little Marah, but I know a place where we can still get some supper. Will you join me?"

Marah hesitated for a second, but took his proffered arm and the two started off with great dignity. Unfortunately, Marah's troublesome petticoat, forgotten for the moment, tripped her once again and she stopped, greatly embarrassed. But Lucien was a fine man of the world and knew what to do. Gallantly he turned his back and Marah stepped out of the perverse garment, tucking it shyly under her arm. Lucien's courtesy knew no bounds and he firmly took the bundle from Marah, stuffing it under his uniform coat.

It was but a step or two to the cafe of the picturesque old Moulin de la Gallette, and the two were presently seated in a quiet corner.

Lucien's hat and sword lay upon the table. A waiter served them with knowing and sympathetic looks. Marah was silent from bewilderment as she looked about her, for the tables in this famous old cafe were crowded even at this late hour and all was gayety. Lucien was silent from admiration as he stared at the girl dazed.

" All the world loves a lover," it is said, and it was apparent to all who cared to take note that here were two people who, from their rapt regard of one another, their adoring glances and bashful silence, were lovers. Many were the smiling nods exhanged and many were the whispered comments. Their waiter ambled to the old pianist over in the corner who bent over his task of sorting his music by the light of sputtering candles. The musician resembled the great, Franz Lizt, with pinched features and flowing grey locks. Even his piano seemed to belong to the long ago with its uneven row of stained ivory keys and the candles on each side to light the music.

The waiter bent close to the ear of the old man, telling him of the lovers who were their guests. He nodded toward their table and the wrinkled face of the musician lighted up as he watched the happy pair. Quickly he rummaged through his stack of music till he found the great old love song by Lizt—"Liebestraum." Gently the fingers strayed over the keyboard as they found the melting chords of the beautiful song. Tenderly he watched the lovers as he played and, lifted beyond his usual ability, the old musician imparted to his playing a subtle charm and beauty that held all in its sway. As the music started, first one table and then another became silent, until all the loud talk and laughter ceased entirely, and all within earshot became absorbed in wonder and delight with the sublime music. With the last chord it was as though a spell had been broken and the old pianist appeared astonished at the thunder of applause and the shouts of brave; encore! The old man managed to get unsteadily upon his feet and waved an arm toward Marah and Lucien. Again the applause broke out with the musician's gesture, louder now than before, but Marah and Lucien were all unconscious of their part in the scene.

Marah's head was bent back and her eyes were rapt as the pianist responded with a repetition of the charming melody played with a depth of feeling he had never before attained. The spell of the music was upon the girl; no wonder love found her heart unguarded and slipped into it this night.

Lucien was affected, too, by the music. But he was more moved by the girl herself, and as intoxicated with Marah's beauty as she was with the music.

As the last note was struck and the thundering applause came again, a great sigh escaped from the girl. Lucien leaned over the table, stretching forth his hand till his fingers lightly touched the hand of the girl. . .

"Marah—you have bewitched me. Many times I have come here to eat, drink and be merry, but never before have I felt so happy as tonight. It is you; you, little Marah. Tell me more about yourself. Where do you live?"

Marah thought a moment sadly and then answered hopelessly:

"Nowhere."

To touch her hand was not enough for Lucien this time. He must lay his hand protectingly over hers and he seemed afraid to ask the next question:

"To whom do you belong?"

There was a gleam of jealousy in his eyes as he waited for her answer. His changed look and manner puzzled Marah. She did not understand its meaning and she answered his last question innocently with:

"Nobody."

A look of triumph lighted the dark eyes in which desire burned as well, and almost fiercely. Lucien slipped his arm around the girl's slender waist. Holding her fast he whispered hoarsely, triumpantly:

"That's a lie! You belong to me!"

Oblivious to the people at the tables around the two pursued their little drama of love to its end. Such public demonstrations were not uncommon in the cafés of Montmartre and constituted just another source of entertainment for the pleasure-loving crowd.

Brutally Lucien forced the girl's head backward till his lips met hers. Their first kiss was strained and savage. The quick love that had come to them seemed to border closely upon hate. So fierce had been Lucien's first advances and so fiery had been Marah's responses that one might question whether these two really loved or repelled each other.

Marah sprang away from Lucien, pounding his chest and then his face with her hard little fists. Again and again she struck him full in the face, till Lucien released her, pushing her from him violently as he did so.

Lucien nursed his injured cheek while he glowered at the girl. Secretly he admired her independence and honored her principles. He remembered her strange assertation that she had killed a man just because that man had attempted to kiss her and Lucien's first doubts that she could have done such a thing were not so positive now as he smarted from the sturdy blows the girl had administered. She was a little spit-fire, he thought, but she was right in fighting against him. She had given him no right to kiss her and, reassured thus, his anger cooled.

Marah's mood, too was undergoing a change. At first furiously angry with this impetuous young man who had dared to force his attentions upon her, even to kissing her, she now watched him stoking his swollen cheek and a touch of sadness and remorse came to the deep blue eyes. Suddenly she became just a child, plaintive and tender, and softly she carressed his hand still held to his cheek. He lowered it as though afraid of her touch and now Marah tenderly caressed his hurt, softly murmuring words of endearment.

The tender fingers, smoothing and soothing his swollen face; the adorable voice, uttering words of love in a low, full-throated contralto, tempted him to again take her into his arms and again force his lips to hers. But the remembrance of the girl's fierce anger made him pause. What sort of a love was this he felt himself fast surrendering to; what sort of a girl was this who first struck him violently and then changed to tenderness? Lucien was fearful; fearful for himself and for her, and he pushed her from him roughly.

"You are the very breath of the sweetness of the flowers and the fire, also, that destroys all in its path; you are all softness one moment and the hardness of stone the next; you are tenderness and love and then on the instant fierceness and hate. You could make a man love you, or choke you, or both!"

In spite of the bitterness of his words he knew that he was getting deeper and deeper in love with her the longer he remained with her. His only hope was to escape and perhaps in time he could forget her and this strange, sudden and overflowing love.

He arose and as he did so his eyes wandered to a clock, reminding him that it was long past the time when he should have been back at the barracks. His soldier's sense of duty and also the thought of the punishment that awaited him caused resentment of this girl to overwhelm him. She was the cause of his breaking the harsh military rules that meant he would suffer later' she was to blame for his present trouble, and he said to Marah, accusingly:

"Do you see the time? I've overstayed my leave and now I'll have to spend three days on bread and water just because of you."

Marah did not understand what he meant. She could not comprehend how she had become the cause for this punishment he mentioned so bitterly and she pouted.

"How am I to blame?" she asked in a low contrite voice. "I am sorry," she continued sadly, "I did not mean to cause you any trouble."

Lucien explained gruffly as he sullenly buckled on his sword:

"I should have been back at barracks long ago and you kept me—that's why you are to blame."

He picked up his hat and set it determinedly upon his head. The quicker he could get away, the better for him, he reasoned, but Marah was looking up to him appealingly. She had no friend to turn to, and here was one who might have helped her leaving with bitter words of accusation upon his lips. She was forlorn, hopelss and afraid. Lucien caught the look in her eyes and it moved him. Because it was impossible to leave her he was exasperated, and almost accusingly he said:

"But I cannot leave you."

The sad, bowed head of the girl came up quickly at his words. She changed like a summer shower and all was sunshine on the instant. Marah, happy, beamed upon him.

But the matter was not settled so easily for Lucien. The girl was a problem for him, and he wondered what to do with her. She offered no suggestion, sitting peacefully watching him with a light in the deep pools of her eyes. He pondered the question for several moments and then an idea came. He called cheerfully to the waiter for the check and said encouragingly to Marah:

"It's all right, little girl; I guess we can make this come out straight—forward march.

They both laughed at his military command and happily walked out arm in arm.

CHAPTER III

"MME. PIGIONIER'S"

Lucien hurried Marah through several dark streets till finally he stopped before a little shop, with leaded windows, upon which the girl read a sign: "Mme. Pigionier's Laundry." In spite of the late hour a toiling figure could be discerned inside bending over an ironing board. Lucien rapped loudly and Mme. Pigionier came slowly to the door with a lighted candle in her hand.

She was a motherly old soul whose toil-worn hands and deeply lined features proclaimed that hard work and worry were her lot in life. She and Lucien were old friends and she listened attentively, with many a side-long glance at the girl, as Lucien rapidly told her his story. He concluded with:

"She has nowhere to go; she's homeless and alone, and it would be a crime to leave her on the streets. She will work for her room and her keep and you'll be nothing out by taking her in."

"It's a likely tale, but strange as it may be, I believe you. But tell me honestly, does the girl belong to you?"

Lucien swore that she did not, and after a long pause Madame told the girl to come in. Marah started to follow her and then realized that this was the parting with her new-found love. She lingered on the door-step looking up into Lucien's face with love-lit eyes. Trembling with passion of her first great love, she stretched out her arms to him as she whispered:

"I forgot to thank you. I don't know what I should have done had it not been for you, and I have no words to tell you how grateful I am. But you will not leave me here alone; you'll come to see me—often, won't you, Lucien?"

He nodded, not trusting his voice to answer this delectable creature who had stolen his heart away. He held her hand lingeringly, loath to let her go. But a call from the hall brought the lovers from their land of dreams and Lucien turned away regretfully as the girl hurried toward the dimly-lighted figure waiting for her impatiently.

Lucien had hardly taken a step, however, before two round, soft arms clasped him in a warm embrace. Marah had returned to the door for one last word, and in the tempest of her feelings she had cast aside all reserve.

How happy he was; she had given herself to him; had kissed him—she was his. He held her tight, but Marah with one last lingering kiss broke away and rushed through the hall to the stairs. Lucien followed close behind, but he paused at the steps and, standing there, strained on tiptoe till he could touch the tips of her fingers. In a moment she was gone.

Lucien stumbled blindly to the street, drunk with love and lost in dreams of his love. He adjusted his coat; he must look his best, even when alone, now that he had a sweetheart. The lump under his uniform coat surprised him, and then, remembering, he pulled out the dainty white petticoat with a smile.

A light appeared at a window above and as Lucien watched, hoping for a last glimpse of his lady love, Marah appeared at the open window. Lucien called to her and tossed the white bundle, which she deftly caught. She stretched forth her arm with a gesture of longing and then blew him a kiss. Lucien saluted her, soldier fashion, stiff and formal, and then, as though afraid to linger longer because of the rash acts he might be tempted to do with his love so near and yet so far, he turned like a flash and ran at top speed down the street.

Marah watched him with a happy smile until he rounded a corner and even then she remained gazing at the point where he had passed from view. She could never see enough of her brave lover, and she was lost in deep reverie. She started from her thoughts upon a sound a good deal like a snort. Mme. Pigionier stood beside her with a stern expression on her face. Madame asked sternly:

"What is that young man to you? Are you sweethearts? He told me that he had met you only tonight. Can you find it possible to love a man in so short a time?"

Marah was confused and embarrassed and knew

not which question to answer first. She glanced at the old lady as she stuttered:

"No—yes—that is, yes, I do love him. I don't care how short the time has been since I have known him; I knew the instant I saw him that I loved him. Oh, Madame," with a plaintive note in her voice, "if you only knew how I worship him."

Mme. Pigionier's susceptible heart melted. It would have been a hard heart indeed that could have remained cold to the appealing presence of this charming girl, even more adorable now with the miracle of her overpowering love shining in her lovely face. Madame sighed heavily and a tear moistened the care-worn cheek as she said simply:

"I am glad."

Marah hesitated an instant, poised like a bird ready to take flight. She looked at Mme. Pigionier eagerly, for something subtle, intangible told her that Madame was more than a friend. She flung herself into the old lady's arms, to be clasped in an ample embrace and, weeping tears of joy and long pent-up longing, Marah knew that here at last she had found a mother.

Mme. Pigionier patted the girl's shoulder in a motherly way, making inarticulate, crooning sounds that spoke to the lonely girl more than words. The old lady gently led Marah away from the window to the center of the room and, standing with her arm protectingly around the girl, she said gently:

"Now, honey, everything is all right. Just you depend on me; I know we are going to get along like mother and daughter—better than a good many. You

You are home now—home, Marah, and this is your room. Do you like it?"

Marah happily surveyed her surroundings. It was a room of ample size, shabby, it is true, but in a picturesque way, and it boasted of a great bay window which gave view upon a panorama of Paris.

The carpet was worn, but swept clean. The chairs were handsome speciments of the furniture-maker's art, with beautiful carvings—prizes to the collector of antiques, but the upholstery was threadbare. In spite of their worn appearance, these chairs seemed to invite one to sit down and be at home, and the spotless, white, knitted doilies upon each lent an air of comfort and hominess to the room. A brilliant figured cover, in which deep red predominated, spread upon the solid old table in the center of the room, added the needed bit of color to offset the sombre dignity of the old furniture.

Mme. Pigionier busied herself in preparing the bed, with its spotless linen, in a small adjoining alcove as Marah drank in the scene with her eyes, too happy to speak.

As Madame returned to the room, Marah flew to her. "Oh, Mother," she started—"may I call you Mother?" At a smiling nod from the old lady, the girl rushed on, the words tumbling from her in a joyous torrent"

"This is really and truly home. I've never seen any room so charming, so dear. Is it really mine? I adore it."

Marah's bubbling enthusiasm struck a responsive

note in Mme. Pigionier's lonely heart. For many years she had lived alone and many were th etimes that she had longed for just such a girl to call her daughter; to cheer her declining years. She lovingly touched the face of the girl as she answered:

"There, there, my little one. Of course it's yours, all yours, and happy I am that I can give you this little room, that I can give you a home." And now the motherly instinct became uppermost. She gently led the girl to the alcove.

"It is late, long past the time when young girls should be in bed and, too, we arise early in Mme. Pigionier's Laundry," she added with a smile. "Into bed with you," she urged briskly, as she helped Marah to prepare, and nothing would induce her to leave till she had tucked the happy girl snugly between the covers and kissed her good night.

Meanwhle, Lucien, breathless from his run, seated himself on a door-step to take stock of the evening's occurrences. One thought alone persisted over all others in his brain and for a long while he was lost in dreams of his sweetheart. A clock striking the hour awoke him from his pleasant memories to the cold realization of the situation facing him. Long overdue at his barracks, he had two alernatives—either to give himself up and take the punishment to be meted out for his breach of discipline, or to try and slip by the guard unnoticed. The latter course was risky, but if successful he would escape the penalty of his night of pleasure, for he knew his comrades would not betray him. On the other hand, if caught in trying to evade the guard his situation would be no worse than if he took the first alternative. It was worth trying, and, his decision made, he hastened toward the barracks.

A sentry paced endlessly up and down outside the walls. At an interval further along, another guard kept the tireless vigil. Lucien crept along in the shadow of the walls, as yet secure, but a loose stone, clattering under his feet, threatened his undoing. The sentry, startled by even so small a noise in the dead silence of the night, peered intently in the direction of the sound.

Lucien crouched in the shadow, but the sentry made out the deeper spot of black that was Lucien's figure and, staring hard, managed to see dimly that the figure was in uniform. Just another of the late ones, he thought. More than once the sentry had been in the same situation. A good fellow, he turned his back and paced in the opposite direction.

Lucien smiled, he would remember this little favor and some day, perhaps, pay the man back. Lucien lost no time in improving his opportunity and leaped lightly toward the top of the wall. It was not very high and his hands found a grip upon the top. It was but a matter of seconds for him to scale the wall, while the friendly sentry watched him with good-humored interest.

Safe! Lucien was happy. He had met his love, spent a joyous evening with her and was back without being caught for being late. He was well toward the great building when the word "Halt!" came sharp and decisive upon the night. No use to run; all was up, and with a disgusted expression Lucien stopped. To be so near safety with the help of the friendly sentry upon the wall, and then to have the cup snatched from his lips. The guard had sprung from nowhere and as Lucien passively handed over his belt and sword the fellow smiled an evil grin. The difference in men, thought Lucien—so it was all through life, he mused as he was placed under arrest and led to the guard room. Three days on bread and water; not so hard except for the three days he would be kept from his sweetheart.

And Marah wondered. Could it be that he had forgotten already? All that first day she had been so busy gathering the threads of the new life before her, she had but fleeting thoughts of her soldier. There were so many nooks and corners to be explored; the kitchen, the dining-room and the work room in the front where across the little counter work for Mme. Pigionier came in and was delivered. Madame's room upstairs and her own which must be rearranged to suit better her tastes; just touches here and there to make it really her own room.

And then the work; she did not mind it. It was not hard, and her strong young arms steadily plied the iron, daintily and cleverly, over the damp clothes. She needed no instructions from Mme. Pigionier, who at once proclaimed Marah a better ironer than she herself with all her experience.

Marah could watch the passing scene of Paris street life through the window as she worked. Smartly dressed men and women; workmen; shop girls, saucy milliners' delivery girls with their great round boxes; a flower vender in quaint costume; a harpist making a precarious living by strumming for the passing crowd; a beggar—

these and many more passed before the delighted eyes of the girl who had within so short a time been set down in this colorful scene from the sleepy quiet of the country. Steadily the iron smoothed out a pretty dress as the girl snatched glances at the busy scene. Many were her thoughts, traveling in a ceaseless circle about one exalted central image—that of her lover.

Night came, to pass in a dreamless sleep earned by the work of the day. But the second morning dawned clouded with half-formed doubts. She had more time, now that the novelty of her new environment had worn off, to give more sober thought to the question that bothered her. Why had Lucien not come to her? Surely last night he could have found an hour.

Busily her troubled thoughts kept time with the steady working of her laundry iron. Lower and lower sank her heart till Mme. Pigionier handed her a letter just delivered. A letter for her; Marah beamed, afluster with excitement. She knew who it was from, even though as she had never before seen his hand-writing, and smiling happily she eagerly tore open the envelope to read over and over again the short note written in a large, masculine scrawl. The girl slowly deciphered the words:

"My Marah: They put me in the jug, but I get out tomorrow. Will see you tomorrow night and we will spend the whole evening together. Lucien."

So he had not forgotten after all. Over and over again Marah read the letter, her first love letter. What did he mean by "jug"? She had no idea, but evidently it was the cause of his absence.

Marah worked diligently at her ironing with the letter on the board beside her. But she could not resist dividing her attention between the words of her lover and the work before her. She ironed with one hand, smoothing the letter out with the other, the better to read it over once again.

Slower, more slowly worked the arm holding the iron, till presently it stopped altogether and Marah stood lost in dreams. Mme. Pigionier, working nearby washing clothes, watched the girl with a knowing eye. Suddenly she cried"

"Marah, Marah, back to work! Is that the way to do, you who are to be of such a help to me, standing there dreaming?"

Marah started guiltily and applied herself industriously to her ironing. Madame smiled indulgently. The girl had captured her heart, and the old lady looked upon Marah as in very truth her daughter. She remembered that she had been young once, and sometimes became lost in dreams, especially when letters came. But Madame did not altogether approve of the soldier lover and in her rôle of motherly protection she tried to give the girl a hint.

"Never love a soldier too well, my dear. It's here today and gone tomorrow—that's their style. Not but that some soldiers are handsome, and worthy and honorable, but their lives are not their own. They belong to their country and if tomorrow their country says that they must pack up with no previous warning and perhaps move clear across the ocean, they have no choice in the matter; they have to go. Then what of you?

Follow your soldier lover?—it is hard, sometimes impossible."

Marah listened to the shrewd remarks, admitting to herself that Madame was right, and the girl's heart was sick within her. Wearily she continued with her work, but her thoughts wandered to Lucien and his letter. She touched it to give her courage and somehow, just the feel of the crinkled paper upon which his dear hand had rested not so long before seemed to bring to her a sense of his strength and protection.

With the day's work done, Marah, curled up in the wide window seat of the big bay window in her room, looked out across the roofs and night life in the streets below. Somewhere in that general direction, mused Marah, was her lover probably dreaming of her, and she tried to project herself to him upon the wings of thought.

A motto hanging upon the wall of the room caught Marah's eye. "Life is Short," it read. "True, oh so ture," murmured Marah, "life is short, but I will make the most of it. Lucien is here now, perhaps he will be stationed here for years, who knows. We love one another—enough; why worry about the future."

All through the following day the thought that Marah had murmured aloud to herself the night before brought her courage. To live in the present; to enjoy the pleasures of today, leaving for tomorrow whatever might transpire then—that was the philosophy of life that Marah was building up for herself and one which she found conforting.

Back in her room Marah was busy preparing to

receive her sweetheart. The clock on the mantle started to strike the hour and Marah, fascinated from the first by this quaint old time-piece, paused in her busy preparations to watch the interesting mechanism. It was a beautiful clock of antique workmanship and made in the shape of a heart. Two pretty little brass figures stood at each side of the dial—a shepherd and shepherdess—and as each hour struck the figures bent forward to kiss in a most lifelike pantomime. As Marah watched she realized the time—eight! Lucien would soon be there.

Marah had planned a delightful little party. She intended it to be an episode of unspoiled happiness; of innocence and poetry; moments to be remembered long after.

Moonlight shone softly through the window, lighting the room dimly as Marah moved around, giving the last touches here and there that women always seem to find necessary upon an occasion like this. She lit a candle and placed it upon the table, where a simple, yet dainty feast had been spread. Candles burned upon the mantel, and a modest bouquet of flowers graced a small wall table. Marah rearranged the table for the hundredth time and then decided the chairs were still too far apart. She moved them as close together as possible with a smile on her lips as she did so, and, giving one last inspection of the table, she hurried to the mirror.

She must look her best. She is anxious as to whether she is pretty enough to hold her brave soldier; whether she is worthy enough of her fine lover. She peered at herself eagerly and made a little grimace of dissatisfaction. It was partly her costume, she decided; the simple, ugly dress she wore did not do her justice. Oh, for a dainty frock of lace and frills and then this would be a party indeed. But what's the use of longing for impossible things; it's her only dress and must do. Perhaps it would look better if she were to unfasten the bodice a little to show more of her round, white throat. A deft movement transformed the stiff, unbecoming neckline of the dress to a modest V, and Marah, after critical examination, decided it an improvement. With a last hasty glance around she fluttered to the window seat to await his coming.

Lucien, free once again of the restraint of the barracks, hurried to his lady love. A comrad walked with him and listened good-humoredly as Lucien described the marvelous perfection of his sweetheart. They reached the little laundry shop and Lucien looked up eagerly to the window, his comrade doing likewise, curious to see this most perfect of all girls, according to Lucien. But Marah had spied the stranger with her sweetheart and had withdrawn, so both the men below were disappointed in their hope of a glimpse of her.

Lucien saluted his comrade and bade him a hasty good night, but the other, in a spirit of teasing, detained the impatient lover, asking for a light. Lucien complied ungraciously; he was anxious to be rid of the fellow and took no pains to hide his feelings. The other smiled knowingly and in an earnest voice warned Lucien:

"It's a fine thing to have a little sweetheart to call upon and while away the lonesome evenings. But no matter how pretty your girl is, you've got to leave her before nine o'clock. Orders are to be at barracks at that time. If you are late this time it will be serious, for the regiment moves, and if they move without you it means a charge of desertion against you."

Lucien nodded dejectedly and entered the hall with feet strangely reluctant, considering that they carried him nearer step by step to his love. He had forgotten for the moment the dreadful spectre of parting which had haunted him ever since he had learned the news of the regiment's departure. His comrade's words recalled his misfortune and how to break the news to Marah, and worse, how they were to exist torn apart at the very beginning of their great love, were problems he quailed to face.

So his step lacked the spring of eagerness as he passed through the hall, and Mme. Pigionier, still working in the laundry, noticed that something was wrong. She called a greeting as he passed, and Lucien saluted absently and without spirit.

"Why have you such a long face?" she asked him. "Anyone would think you were going to a funeral instead of to your sweetheart to see the way you lag on the way and the sour looks you bring along."

Lucien answered her in a woe-begone tone:

"It's cause enough I have for a long face. We've been ordered to Algiers for three years, and we leave tonight. That's not very good news and you can't blame me for not rushing to Marah with the tidings, can you?"

Mme. Pigionier shook her head sympathetically. "Dear, dear, what a pity," she said and then brightly, " but there will be plenty of girls in Algiers."

"And such girls," she continued, accompanying her words with a vivid pantomime as she talked: "Such girls; dark eyes, glossy black hair, such divine figures and, oh, such a wonderful way of dancing!" With that she mimicked an Arab dance with witty clumsiness.

The old lady's antics were really laughable, and Lucien, for all his sadness, laughed, for laughter was a habit with him anyway.

Mme. Pigionier continued her performance, now that her audience approved, and went through the movments of a voluptuous Oriental dance. Her performance was marvelous, but alas!—she was old and homely. At last she stopped close to the wanely smiling young man and said:

"You see, great things are in store for you. You will soon forget Paris and all your friends. What between the pretty girls who await you and their charming dances—oh," and she kissed the tips of her fingers, opening them as she did so with a gesture of flinging the kiss to the winds.

Lucien laughed again, but then his thoughts returned to Marah and he said sadly:

"There may be girls in Algiers and they may know how to dance, but they will not be Marah. No one can compare with her, and I can never forget her. How can you act so, making me laugh when you know how sad I am and how sad she will be?"

Mme. Pigionier shrugged. She was sorry in a way, but glad too, for she figured that once out of the way, Lucien would in time be forgotten by Marah. In her motherly position toward the girl she resolved that with

Lucien gone there would be no more soldier lovers! So more to tease him, Madame answered:

"Don't worry about Marah. She will get over the sdness of parting." And then with a sly wink she added maliciously: "And don't forget, there will be plenty of soldiers left in Paris."

"Soldiers in Paris"—the words hit him like a blow. He had not thought of them before, and the idea brought thoughts that roused his intense jealousy. He paled and his hands clinched. His eyes blazed as though already he beheld his hated rivals. A pretty girl like Marah would not lack suitors and Lucien was furious. Without another word he turned and rapidly mounted the stairs.

The old lady stared after him in amazement. My, what a rude fellow, she thought. She had not meant to wound him so badly, and she was sorry, especially as the poor boy was leaving and her Marah was safe. Perhaps she should not have been so outspoken, but it was said and the old lady shrugged as she went back to work.

Lucien mounted the stair slowly. At Marah's door he paused to pull himself together. With an effort he formed a smile, for he was determined that the evening should pass happily. He would not tell her till the very moment of parting and till then there must be nothing to mar the joy of the little party. To create the proper mood of gayety he began to sing softly the musketeer song which had been their introduction:

> "When I was a musketeer,
> A ron-ron-ron!"

The Divine Woman

With the first notes Marah turned from her task of winding the lover's clock on the mantel, a light of gladness shing in her eyes. She watched the door in ecstasy and as Lucien, forcing himself to be gay, came into the room still singing, she rushed to meet him.

There was a pagan joyousness in her movements and a smouldering passion that all but swept Lucien off his feet as she leaped into his arms. Their lips met in a long kiss as the man held her close to his heart.

Marah was the first to withdraw. Pressing her hands upon his chest, she thrust him away and then held him at arm's length as she drank in the picture of her soldier. And it was a brave and handsome picture he made. In his natty, well-fitting uniform which set off to perfection his broad-shouldered, tall form, Lucien was from the heels of his shoes to the crown of his head the soldier. His walk had the easy swing that came from the rhythm of the march, and his quick, precise movements and the smart manner of his carriage were the result of his military training.

His hair, with a wave that was the envy of many a girl, was Marah's greatest delight, and she seemed to take a particular pleasure in rumpling it and then patting it back in place. Steady, honest eyes of brown, eyes ever snapping with the fun from under a broad brow; a strong, straight nose; a wide, pleasant mouth, and a round, determined chin completed a countenance which more than one girl had found attractive. A small mustache should not be left out of the picture. It was the style for the men of Lucien's regiment to affect such a mustache, and the mode was to keep it clipped short just covering the lip. It rather added to Lucien's dashing appearance, and Marah greatly admired it.

For a long moment she held him at arm's length, with her hands on his shoulders. Not a word had been spoken till Marah now said:

"Lucien," dwelling fondly on the name, "how glad I am you have come. I've waited, and the time has seemed so long. And now that you are here, make yourself at home. Give me your hat and that horrid sword.

Lucien smiled as he handed her his hat and un-buckled his sword. It was a delight to the girl to wait on him, and she tripped happily to the mantel, where she laid the sword and hat alongside the clock which she remembered she had not finished winding.

Over her shoulder she laughed archly at her lover, as he stood in the middle of the room, watching her intently with a strained look upon his face. Marah's small act of winding the clock had reminded him of the fatal hour of parting, even now so near. He had almost forgotten, and it seemed an irony of fate that she should remind him.

Marah noticed for the first time that Lucien seemed distant and reserved. As yet he had said no word to her, and how peculiar he looked as he watched her.

"What is it, Lucien, are you not well? You have not spoken to me; haven't said you are glad to see me, and you look at me so crossly."

Lucien, who had been on the point of telling her the bad news, decided against it and by a supreme effort manged a gay note as he answered:

"You are so beautiful, Marah dear, that you took

my breath away, so that I could not speak. And as for being cross, it was not for you, but for the time, as I realized how short the hours before we would again have to part."

"Don't bother about the time yet, Lucien, but come, let us have our party and enjoy the hours before they slip away."

Happy as a child, she took his hand and led him to the table. She was pleased with her success as a hostess and very proud of her little feast. As Lucien looked over the table he was really surprised. The repast was arranged with a dainty tastefulness that was an art in itself. One's appitite was whetted just by the tempting way the good things were served.

Lucien was loud in his praise, and many were the extravagant compliments he made. He looked around the cozy little room and admired one thing after another. Coming to the little table containing the flowers he begged that he might have one, and Marah was forced to stand on tiptoe to place it in his lapel. He teased her by kissing her hands as she stove to pin the little flower fast.

He had not forgotten a gift for his sweetheart, and with a great show of unconcern he drew a necklace from his pocket. It was obviously cheap and vulgar, but to Marah it was magnificent. As he clasped it about her neck, he said in a bantering tone:

"There, you've been teasing for a present; now I hope you're happy."

She tormented him by little pecking kisses as he fumbled with the catch, so that he scarcely was able to clasp the trinket. Indignantly Marah answered him, as he finally manged to secure it:

"The very idea, as if I would ask you for a gift. But there, you naughty boy, as long as you have brought it, I will wear it as a great favor to you." She said it in a archly bantering manner, and before he could protest, she continued: "And it's beautiful, Lucien—how can I thank you! Let me see how it looks."

She hurried to the mirror and preened herself before the glass. Twisting the necklace first this way, then that, she examined the different effects, and it was very apparent that Marah was a vain little thing.

Lucien watched her happily, but in doing so his gaze encountered the abominable clock, and again he was reminded of the evil hour. Inexorable the clock had been ticking away the time, and it was already close to nine o'clock, with the little party hardly begun.

Lucien's heart sank, and the laughter of the moment before was like ashes in his mouth. Now was the time to tell her and have done with it; why try to force a gayety he could not genuinely feel. But looking at her, bubbling with radiant happiness, was too much for him; he could not bring himself to the task, for it would be like slaying a tender, innocent thing to kill her joy now. He would wait till the very hour struck and then . . . .

Marah called to him gaily: "Wait, Lucien, wait just a moment. I have another surprise for you—a wonderful surprise." She fairly flew to the cupboard and flung open the door. From its depths she withdrew her treasure and held it proudly for his inspection. It was a bottle, not of a famous vintage, but at lest ripe with age as was testified by the cobwebs which covered it.

Lucien critically examined the label and nodded approval. Marah, in the extreme of her joy, asked if it were not fit to be kissed, and suiting action to the word, she pressed the bottle to her lips ecstatically. The result was a smudge over her pretty mouth from the cobwebs and dust which covered the bottle. Lucien scolded her, for like a naughty child she had dirtied her face. He must clean it, and bidding her stand before him, he wiped the smudge away with a napkin.

The girl's close proximity overpowered him, and snatching her roughly to him, he covered her face with kisses. Holding her tightly, almost smothering her with his bearlike embrace, he laid his head close to hers.

That detestable clock—will he always be reminded of his short hour of happiness? As he laid his head close to the adorable face of his loved-one, his eyes over her shoulder had unconsciously wandered to the clock, whose hands, like the finger of fate, pointed the brief interval of time still remaining to him.

His eyes narrowed momentarily, but he again forced himself to act the part of the happy merrymaker. He would not let a silly clock spoil the brief moments of happiness still left to them, and so that he might drown his wretchedness, he went to the other extreme of gayety. He swung the laughing girl to his shoulder and marched around the room, singing his soldier song:

"When I was a musketeer,
A ron-ron-ron!"

Marah joined in the singing, beating time prettily

as they progressed around the room. They were both carried away by the joy of each other's presence and the singing, and Lucien rode the top of the wave of happiness with no thought of the dread hour of nine. Striding across the room, he approached the table and with a debonair flouish swung the flushed girl down into the chair and, with a merry bow, took the other.

With chairs touching, so close together that they interfered with one another as they ate, the little banquet started. At each small accident, when an elbow or an arm jolted the morsel of food from the fork being raised to mouth, there was a happy burst of laughter. They must both drink from the same glass upon Marah's insistance, and Marah, having tasted first, passed the glass to Lucien. He kissed the place where her lips had touched, and sipped tenderly.

Marah thought him adorable, the little action with the glass seemed to her simple soul to show how greatly he loved her, and so, in a low voice, trembling with emotion, she said:

"Lucien dear, I'm so happy. Too happy. I could sing and dance and do all kinds of silly things just because the happiness is so great, there is no room for it inside, and it just bubbles over. Sometimes I think it can't last—some day something will take you from me, and that would break my heart."

Marah sighed at the thought, but quickly the mood passed, and she smiled again. Why think of unpleasant things; were they not together now and happy? She had already resolved to live in the present, and the present was all happiness, so she laughed.

She had not noticed how Lucien's face had clouded at her words. Why must he be reminded at every turn. Just when he was entering into the spirit of the gay evening, just when he had completely forgotten the hour of parting that approached them like doom, he had to again be brought up sharply to a realization of the facts. It seemed that fate would not let him forget. Now is the time to tell her, and he started to break the news gently:

"Some day I may have to leave you . . . ."

His heart failed him again, and his voice trailed off into silence, Marah remember what Mme. Pigionier had told her—that soldiers are here today and gone tomorrow. Therefore, her heart was sick and she asked why he had said that. Now, if ever, was the time for Lucien to break the news, but again he hesitated to come out frankly with the truth. He tried to make it easier for her by being casual, and passed off his previous statement by remarking in the most matter-of-fact way that all lovers must part sometime.

Marah's her hot temper quick to spring up, thought his tone too carefree in speaking of so solemn and holy a thing as she considered their love to be. She believed for the moment that he was making light of her love, and rather than to let him see that he had wounded her, she covered her hurt by adoptin as careless a tone as he. She intended to prick him with the dart of her sharp tongue, wounding him as he had her, so, gaily breaking a piece of bread, with a great show of unconcern, she answered with bravado:

"Well, if, as you say, lovers must part sometime, I suppose it must be. But how fortunate that there are plenty of other soldiers in Paris."

Almost the very words that Mme. Pigionier had used. Marah had touched his sorest spot, had said the one thing he could not bear to hear. Jealousy made him boil with anger, and he pushed his chair roughly from the table. Without a word he went from the table and stalked with angry strides to the mantel. Sulkily and still silent, he took his sword and buckled it violently, cramming his hat upon his head. Still without speaking, without so much as a glance in her direction, he strode resentfully to the door.

Marah was dumbfounded when he scraped his chair from the table. She had not meant to hurt him, and she could not understand why he should be so angry over so small a matter as her teasing remark, made in fun. She stared at him incredulously; surely he would not have the will power to leave her thus. But now his hand was on the knob of the door and he had said nothing nor even looked her way. He turned the knob; the door was open!

Desperately Marah called to him: "Lucien! Lucien! Don't go that way. How could you? What have I done that you should treat me so?"

Lucien turned, the note of pathos in her voice was more than he could bear. He lost all courage to go and unresisting allowed Marah to lead him by the hand back into the room. Triumphantly she unbuckled his sword and reached on tiptoe for his hat. Still standing thus, she rumpled his hair and patted his cheek, smiling into his eyes. He watched her sadly as she went to the mantel with his hat and sword.

Lucien was a little angry—angry with himself and disgusted too. He had awakened to the fact that he had not the strength to leave like a man; had not the courage to tell her frankly that this was the end to their romance. He was beginning to be afraid of himself, because she was possessing him utterly; because he appreciated that he was but clay in her hands.

With a pretty air of possession Marah returned to him and confidently put her arm through his, leading him to the wide seat in the bay window. Giving him a little push, she forced him to sit down and laughed happily at his docility. She held him a prisoner; never was any man more under the power of a woman contentedly with her head nestling on his breast. In contrast to her happiness he was dumb and silent, with a sad, forlorn look upon his face.

Marah failed to notice how sad and silent he was. She took his lassitude as coming perhaps from a hard day of work. Possibly he was still resentful of the teasing which drove him toward the door before. So she shook him as though he were a naughty child, and then, as though to excuse her momentary harshness, she snuggled still closer to him, and her soft warm arms crept about his neck. She was all innocence as she surrendered herself to him and whispered:

"Lucien, my love, this is bliss. Promise to hold me always thus; promise never to leave me."

The man was stricken and silent. She had asked for a promise he could not give. He understood too late that he should never have allowed things to go so far. He was not his own master, he "belonged" to his country, and as a soldier of France he must obey a call that recognized no human emotion, that tolerated no sentiments save that of the one cardinal requirement of the soldier—duty!

Too late!—ah yes, too late, for this girl had given herself to him without restraint and to tear himself from her now would be to wound her whom it should be his first duty to protect.

Marah covered his face with little teasing kisses. She was altogether adorable and it was more than his will could withstand. He crushed her to him. In the midst of his ecstasy the little clock began to strike, the pretty figures kissing in so life-like manner. Stricken, he listened to the chimes—tolling, tolling—almost a death knell. Dumbly he counted—seven—eight—nine! It was the hour of parting!

Marah sensed the tension and believed that he was fighting against his passion for her. She could not understand that his struggle was deeper than that. She fought to hold him and almost succeeded, but Lucien's long training could not be conquered so easily, and duty forced him to tear himself from her. He rushed to the mantel as one fleeing from a great danger.

In frenzied haste, lest his passion master him, Lucien took his hat and sword. Again he approached the door, a door that once closed, he felt, would shut from his life forever all sunshine and happiness. His steps lingered and irresistably his eyes were drawn toward the girl.

She was standing with her eyes closed, the very embodiment of love and passion. And still with her eyes closed she threw out her hands to him and murmured: "Lucien!—come back!"

He knew that she wanted him—needed him. He still had time to reach the barracks. To stay meant disgrace, imprisonment if he should be found, for France searched out her deserters from the Army relentlessly. He knew that he would never be secure no matter how well he might hide. But her voice!—the vision of her dumbly standing there, entreating him to stay. It was enough!—he surrendered!—what matter duty when he had—Marah!

The lights of Paris twinkled across the house tops as the man and girl gazed from the window locked, in one another's arms. The little clock was striking again and again Lucien unconsciously counted—ten—eleven—twelve. Midnight!—can it be that the hours have flown so fast. It was only a moment ago, it seemed, that he had counted the chimes. The chimes. The thought brought with it a twinge of regret and he glanced down at the childish figure curled up and dozing in his arms. Tenderly he laid the sleeping figure on the seat as he slipped a pillow under the tousled head.

He was troubled still, the devilish clock striking the hour brought back again his sense of guilt. Restlessly he walked to the mantel and peered closely at the small dial as though to thus confirm the audible proclamation of the time. Yes, twelve, there could be no mistake, and Lucien reached his hand toward the clock. He hated the thing with its relentless ticking and was on the point of silencing it for all time, but he immediately was ashamed of his petulance.

There beside the clock on the mantel were his sword and cap and he touched them regretfully. His heart was breaking at the thought that he had not the right to wear them anymore. But, ah!—perhaps after all it might not be too late. By some chance the regiment may have been delayed and if he should hurry . . . .

He buckled on his sword with eager haste; he put on his hat and started for the door, but before he reached it a stir from the sleeping figure arrested him. Sleepily she called: "Lucien, where are you?"

Guiltily he unbuckled his sword and snatched off his hat as though caught in a dishonorable act. He went to her quickly and hiding his agitation behind a smile looked down upon her as she drawsily opened her eyes and beamed up at him.

"Sing to me Lucien," she said, "sing the funny little soldier song."

Why must she ask for that song. Of all songs not that. But she was insistent and he began mournfully:
>"When I was a musketeer
>A ron—rom—ron"

The words almost choked him, but the sweet contentment on the face so dear to him, made it easier and his voice softened. Sorrow and regret stalked in his eyes as he sang, while Marah beat time sleepily. Soon the song brought courage and he sang almost bravely:
>"When I was a musketeer
>How brave a lad was I"

The words stung him to a realization that he was not a brave lad any more. His voice broke, he faltered, but he would not let his courage desert him and he braced himself anew and began to sing again, this time with exaggerated spirit. It was as though he were defying destiny.

Meanwhile, drowsiness had again overcome Marah and she beat with less and less spirit. Presently the hand fell to her side; she was asleep!

With a long lingering look at the sleeping girl, Lucien back softly away, picking up his sword and hat from the floor. "Still time! Still time," the thought throbed in his brain like the tolling of a bell. If he could only get to the door, but befoe he was half way there, the girl stirred again and in her sleep murmured his name: "Lucien."

It was the last straw, it seemed almost like the call of fate and his name, uttered all unconsciously by the trusting girl, made him aware of his unworthy act. What a cur he would be, he thought, to steal like a thief away from her. Shaking himself as though ridding himself of a hideous dream, he hastily put sword and hat back on the mantel and softly returned to the sleeping figure.

Fondly he looked down upon her. Her love consoled him. Surely, while he had her all would be well with him.

As though the intensity of his feelings pierced through the fabric of her sleep, the girl opened her eyes. Aware of his presence, a calm of utter contentment spread over her features and she smiled up at him. She raised her arms to him and he knelt down beside her, burying his head upon her breast.

CHAPTER IV

"CAUGHT"

It was evening and all Paris was mantled in a white robe of snow. A man slinked furtively along in the shadow of the houses, pausing ever and anon to peer fearfully behind him. He was like some haunted animal.

He was dressed in a long coat and slouch hat. The hat pulled down over his eyes; the collar of his coat turned up so that only a small white spot could be seen of his face. Even so, he turned his head aside upon meeting every passerby.

He paused at a door and knocked stealthily, glancing right and left as though ready to run at the smallest alarm. In the dim light from the window the stranger may be recognized if one could get close enough. He is Lucien. Lucien, the hunted; the deserter from the army who must disguise himself in civilian clothes and wander through the streets of Paris a fugitive; who must look upon all men as his enemies. There is a reward upon his head and he dare trust no one.

The timid knock was repeated and Mme. Pigionier did not more than glance at the door in annoyance. She continued placidly with her work. She sprinkled the clothes on her ironing board by taking a mouthful of water from a jug and ejecting it in a fine spray through her pursed lips.

Madame was disgusted with Lucien and took her own time in going to the door. Only upon his third knock, which in the man's urgency there was imparted almost a desperate ring to the sound, did Madame slowly go to answer it.

As Lucien slinked in, dodging behind the old lady, she scornfully regarded him and slammed the door shut irritably.

Lucien took off his hat and shook the snow from it. It was a changed Lucien. Gone was the trim mustache, gone also the nonchalant manner. His hair was long and unkempt, his cheeks hollow and his eyes sunken and blood-shot. The acid of his crime had eaten into his very soul and made him a beaten, furtive, bitter man. He was physically weakened, too, and his thin form now shivered from the cold. He looked around fearfully as though expecting a hidden enemy even here and in a hoarse whisper asked:

"Where is Marah?"

Mme. Pigionier, never very favorable toward Lucien in his attentions to Marah, was now his bitterest opponent and never missed a chance to wound him. She knew before she spoke that her answer would hurt him so it was with some satisfaction that she said:

"Why do you always ask where Marah is? What

business is it of yours where she is? She is not accountable to you, but if you must know, I sent her with some laundry to the Theatre Carre."

Madame finished with a satisfied air and if it was her desire to arouse Lucien's jealousy she certainly accomplished her end. But the man's jealousy, which at one time would have made him purple with rage, now was a pitiful thing to see. It made him lugubrious and his tone was not one of anger, but a querulous whine as he said:

"The theatre, why do you send her there? It's bad for her, it gets wrong ideas into her head. It's always the theatre nowadays; she is forever talking about it. She wants to be an actress and you make it worse by sending her there with laundry."

The old lady listened to his tirade with a malicious smile. She found it a great satisfaction to annoy him. Lucien before was an unwelcome suitor for Marah's favors; now a positive handicap. Mme. Pigionier meant that he should not have all of Marah's youth and love. The girl had endeared herself more and more with each passing day with the old lady and Madame looked upon Marah as her own flesh and blood. She could not tolerate this whimpering, good-for-nothing man who was spoiling the girl's life and if a sharp tongue would drive him away, Mme. Pigionier would accomplish it. She answered his last remark with great asperity of manner:

"Actress, eh! Well, if that ever happens, and I see no reason why it should not, it will be the end of you. If she gets her chance and makes good on the stage she can't have you hanging around. You'd be a drag upon her and anyway, once she gets on the stage and meets some of those fine actors, your doom is sealed. She'll want nothing more to do with a thing like you."

The old lady's words cut like a whip, but Lucien had lost all spirit to resent the words themselves or the tone and manner of their speaking. The only thing that hurt him was the fact that what Madame said about losing Marah had a basis of fact and the thought tormented him. The pain of it made him sullen and, in a childish way, angry, and with a gesture as near of violence as he could accomplish in his present pitiful state he snatched a bottle of cognac from the pocket of his coat and slammed it down upon the table.

Cognac was his consolation and his undoing. Every penny he could get his hands on went for the fiery liquid and it made him sodden and morose, each bottle crowding him definitely a little lower in the rapid decline of his manhood.

Mme. Pigionier looked contemtuously from the bottle to Lucien. She thought that perhaps that might be one way of getting rid of him—if he would only drink it fast enough. She watched him with disgust and deep dislike in her eyes as he went to a cupboard at the rear of the laundry.

In his rambling way, Lucien had remembered his uniform. Dimly it recalled a glorious past that now seemed years ago. In back of a pile of laundry in the cupboard Lucien drew forth his uniform. It was there that he had hidden the telltale evidence of his desertion from the army. His hat and sword, his shoes and uniform followed in order, and as each article was withdrawn from its hiding place the man fondled it as though it belonged to one who had departed this life. In a way, these things were the belongings of one long dead; they had never been worn by him who now fingered them lovingly; they were the possession of the ghost of this hopeless wreck of humanity. Lucien laid them all out upon the table—these symbols of his former glory.

Lucien stood, swaying slightly, and surveyed with water eye the only links now remaining to connect his present wretched plight to a better time, when he had been free to look every man fearlessly in the eye. Some idea of the depths to which he had sunk glimmered in his mind as he contemplated his treasures. It was a risk to keep them, for if found, their mute evidence alone would be enough to convict him. Prudence dictated the utter destruction, but Lucien could not make the sacrifice. He was recalled from his dismal musing by the sharp voice of Mme. Pigionier. Pursuing the advantage she had gained with her taunt that Marah would leave him, the old lady continued in the same strain:

"What good is that uniform to you now? You cannot wear it, and so impose upon a susceptible girl any longer. Why don't you be off with you. You are only a handicap to her. The longer you stay here the harder it will be for her to get on. You are going to lose out in the end. You are going to lose her some day as surely as others have lost, who have no more to offer than you."

Lucien was utterly crushed, and cringed under the frank and bitter words. He turned from the old woman and blindly walked to the chair upon which he had flung his coat. His hand convulsively grasped the back of the chair; he was suffering now and in a welter of self-pity, in which bitter tears streamed down his cheeks, he determined to go away. It was the first decisive thing he had done in many a day and even now his mind was vacillating. But Madame had kindled a small spark of manhood that still smouldered in him and with a shuddering effort of his will he put on his overcoat. Carefully he turned up the collar as was his wont and pulled the slouch hat far down over his eyes. With quick, determined steps as though to get outside before he could change his mind, he went to the door and disappeared in the night.

Mme. Pigionier watched him narrowly. She had expected that this was just another whim and that before he reached the door he would turn like a whipped cur. His movement of determination was a surprise to her and before she could say a word he had gone. She half regretted her words; perhaps she had been unnecessarily unkind, she thought as she looked after him pityingly, but what she did was for Marah's benefit. Ah, well; perhaps it was for the best and with a typical shrug Madame went back to her work.

Meanwhile, Lucien dodging along the dark streets, hiding in door-ways whenever a foot-step was heard, found that his fine determination to leave Marah forever was oozing from him. Perhaps if he could do something to win her approval he would be more welcome and as he made his way, choosing the darkest streets and the darker side of each, he was trying to think of something he might do to re-establish himself.

A lighted shop across the way brought a happy idea. That is what would please Marah—clothes. That is what she needed' pretty clothes. It was a wrench for him to take the terrifying step of exposing himself in the brightly-lighted shop, where, in his fear-crazed mind, he was liable to be recognized and arrested. But after many a flase start he finally screwed his courage up and dodged through the door.

It was a small, ill-kept shop, with cheap and dowdy merchandise, but to the simple taste of this man, tottering on the outer rim of society, the stock was dazzling. Lucien was appalled as he enquired the price of first one garment and then another. Finally he reached a simple, but gaudy little dress the cost of which came closer to his means. Still it was far beyond the limits of his strained financial resources and he bargained earnestly with the excitable merchant.

The man named a price, one of a series which had slid down the scale with painful slowness for Lucien. The figure just named was the merchant's last and he said so shortly. Lucien put his hand into his pockets and glanced furtively at the few small coins, and hopelessly small sum of his entire fortune. He had not enough money by a wide margin to pay the last price named and Lucien pleaded with the storekeeper begging the man to let him have the dress for the amount in his hand.

The man became impatient. He was used to bargaining with customers, for his shop was in a neighborhood where to haggle in making a puchase was second nature, and where the first price was tacitly agreed as not the selling price by both buyer and seller.

But this man had bargained with him beyond all reason and already the merchant had lowered his price considerably under the figure for which he would ordinarily have sold. He was therefore obdurate to all Lucien's arguments and pleas and Lucien became discouraged and wretched.

A more prosperous customer entered at this point and the merchant hastened away, leaving Lucien forlornly fingering the prize he had battled for so stoutly and—lost.

The new customer did not quibble too much and the merchant gave him his entire attention, glad to be rid of the shabby, unfortunate man who had made such unreasonable and ridiculous offers for his valuable wares.

Regretfully Lucien laid aside the dress and watched with envy the spendthrift way in which the other customer bought. A dress with spangles; a glittering frock— one, two, three dresses, more than any girl should need thought poor Lucien. The customer purchased with seeming utter disregard to what Lucien's mind must be a fortune which his selections cost.

Lucien rebelled at life's unequality. Other men could buy many dresses for their sweethearts while he could not buy even so poor a one as this on the table in front of him. The merchant had forgotten his very existence. Both he and his customer were engrossed in the business at hand and Lucien was as free as if alone in the shop.

It was a desperate step, but the only one; a step he would not have dreamed of taking awhile back, but one

which came easily in his present low estate. He seized
the dress and stuffed it under his coat with an impulsive,
defiant gesture.

It was but a jump to the door and he had gone
in a flash. The slamming of the door reminded the
merchant of his troublesome customer. He was too
occupied at the moment to give more than passing tten-
tion to Lucien's abrupt departure, but a vague suspicion
prompted him to close the deal at hand with unusual
despatch. He rummaged among the things on the table
where he left Lucien, and his suspicions were confirmed;
the dress was missing!

Lucien hurried down the dark street from the
shop, secure in his belief that the merchant would not
discover his loss until he, Lucien, was safely away. But
in this he reckoned without taking into consideration
the shrewdness and suspicion of the store-keeper who
had caught a glimpse of Lucien's hurrying figure and
dogged his steps as a hunter stalks his prey.

Lucien reached the laundry and rapped with more
than usual assurance. Mme. Pigionier met him with
supreme disdain and disgust written upon her features.

Just as she thought. Not rid of him after all. Like
a bad penny he had turned up again.

"Where's Marah?" Lucien asked and then realized
that was the question which started Madame off before.
Without waiting for her answer, he hastened to say:

"See what I've brought for her?—is it not beautiful?"
and he held the cheap little dress up for Madame's inspection. But Mme. Pigionier had washed and ironed

too may dresses to be fooled by this gaudy imitation of quality, so she sniffed, but made no comment as she went back to her work. She watched without speaking as Lucien with more spirit than he had displayed in many a day, arranged his prize.

With elaborate care Lucien draped the dress upon a chair, with the sleeves placed along the arms. Behind this he placed a broom surmounted by an Apache tam so that the latter came just above the back of the chair. He stepped back to survey his handiwork and Madame at her iron-board had to smile in spite of herself at the grotesque, but very lifelike, dummy. The clock striking midnight reminded Lucien that it was long past a reasonable time to expect Marah's return. Madame, too had become alarmed and the two waited anxiously with feelings for once closely akin.

Marah had left the laundry with her basket of clothes with a light heart. She had often made deliveries to the Theatre Carre and was fascinated by the sights and sounds of the theatre. It was something in the nature of a holiday, therefore, whenever Mme. Pigionier directed her to take the basket to the theatre. It was her habit on such excursions to find a dark place in the wings which extended upon each side of the stage and, snugly ensconced there to watch the rehearsal or the performance whichever might be taking place out on the brilliantly-lighted stage.

She arrived upon this occasion after the play had opened. To reach her favorite vantage point it was necessary for her to slip by Gigi, the call-boy. The boy part was a misnomer, for he was a man in fact; a little gnome-like figure and a quaint character. His face was deeply-lined and the most prominent feature was his long nose which Marah had often likened to a carrot. He wore a quaint old-fashioned stock and a skull cap with a tassel. He was a tyrant in his rule of the stage and if he should spy Marah she would be banished forthwith as she had learned to her sorrow at numerous previous occasions.Marah crept along cautiouly; now she was almost past Gigi whose entire attention was centered on the action taking place out in front. Safely past, she crouched in her dark corner with a sigh of relief and contentment.

The scene before her on the stage was one of romance and beauty, Beneath a great cherry tree, white with blossoms, a lady was seated with her lover. Beyond them, at an angle to the stage, Marah could just see the boxes where people in evening clothes were seated watching the performance.

The sage was the scene of passion and idealism such as one could never find in real life. It was a play designed to appeal to the eyes as well as the mind, and the stage settings and costumes were magnificent. Mme. Paulette, the beautiful star wore an especially handsome costume that fairly dazzled poor little Marah. Her breath was taken away by its splendor. Clad in this gorgeous costume, a gown of silver cloth with irridescent crystals, Mme. Paulette listened at languid ease to the voice of her lover who knelt at her feet, pouring out his passionate love in exaggerated phrases such as no real lover would ever have the presence of mind to think of. He finished and bent to kiss the hem of her robe as white petals dropped from the cherry tree upon them.

Marah fairly absorbed the scene, drinking in the love speech. She was living the play enacted before her and tears came to her eyes.

Gigi turned and by chance his glance fell upon the hapless Marah. Now many times had he forbidden the little laundress to come into the wings; how often had he driven her from her corner. He shook his head impatiently and started toward her.

Marah did not see him coming. Her head was thrown back, her hands clasped in exactly the posture of the leading woman on the stage. The girl had seen the play before and had studied every move of the star. She could imitate perfectly the smallest action of the great actress. Marah, lost in the ecstasy of the part, continued to react the scene on the stage. She reproduced gesture for gesture, pose for pose, the actions of the star.

Gigi reached her side unnoticed. He touched her shoulder. Marah turned to him and Gigi saw that there were tears on her cheeks—real tears, for she had lost herself in the emotion of the play. Being an inherent actress, Marah brushed the tears away and smiled upon the little man. She explained in pantomime that she was just imitating the scene on the stage.

Gigi shook his finger at her scoldingly, but indulgently. He would not listen to her pleas and insisted that she must go. Obediently, but reluctantly, with a long last look at the pretty scene on the stage beyond,

Marah picked up her laundry basket and trudged up the stairs which led to the dressing rooms.

All the magic had gone from Marah now that she has been ordered from the stage. The laundry was for Mme. Paulette and Marah drearily bore the heavy basket to the star's dressing room.

She removed the laundry slowly bending wearily to the task and arranged it in neat piles. Her task finished, she looked around the room. She admired Paulette's various costumes, carelessly thrown upon chairs, going from one to another touching and fingering each. Finally in her circuit of the room, Marah reached the star's luxurious dressing table with its great triple mirror and rich, jewel-studded toilet service.

Heedlessly left in the litter of odds and ends heaped upon the dressing table, Marah saw something which electrified her. It was a beautiful necklace of diamonds that glittered and sparkled, flashing fire from the lights of the room.

Marah stared at the necklace fascinated. She picked it up and moved it from side to side to see the diamonds sparkle. The girl was wearing Lucien's cheap little trinket; the neckless she thought so handsome when he gave it to her. Now she held the two side by side and laughed aloud.

Quickly Marah placed the stunning diamond necklace around her pretty white throat, admiring the effect and looking at herself in the mirror. She held Lucien's gee-gaw beside the rich jewels and noted again the difference. The cheap bauble evoked an expression of disgust and she flung it from her across the room where it landed, a sorry, battered heap, in the corner.

Marah turned again to the mirror and viewed the sparkling jewels from various angles. At this point the door opened and Paulette entered. Marah saw her in the mirror with a start of horror, fingering the necklace guiltily.

For a second the actress did not notice that Marah wore her necklace. Then, with a gasp of indignation, with flashing, angry eyes, she rushed at the girl. Her hands clutched like claws and she grasped Marah roughly by the arm as she reached toward the girl's throat to snatch away her jewels.

Marah warded off the attack easily and drew back with dignity. She deliberately removed the necklace and dropped it with a careless gesture of unconcern upon the table, eyeing the flushed and angry actress with scorn.

Paulette in turn drew herself up and surveyed the girl slowly from head to toe with a contemptuous sneer. She was a woman of no refinement and her crude speech revealed her ill breeding.

"Well, you, what do you mean by putting my jewels around your dirty neck. You, my laundress, no more than a common nobody to dare to even touch my jewels. Don't you know they are not meant for swine . . . ."

But she got no further. Marah broke in upon the violent tirade with words as vehement as the other's.

"My neck is not dirty; if you will take the powder off yours you will find that mine is cleaner than your own wrinkled neck." Picking up the diamonds, with a gesture of violent temper, and holding them to her throat, Marah continued witheringly.

"See, how they sparkle when worn by one who is worthy of them? I am born for these jewels—you to be the laundress!" With that, Marah threw the necklace carelessly back upon the table.

The loud voices had attracted attention and Carre had entered the room unnoticed by either Marah or the agitated actress. He had witnessed most of the scene and appreciated Marah's spirit and pluck and in especial, the biting sarcasm of her retort.

As Paulette stood stunned and speechless by Marah's audacity, Carre slowly, with a twinkle in his eye, approached the angry girl.

Marah had often obtained glimpses of Carre upon her visits at the theatre. Even since the episode at her mother's home, she had been at a loss how to act with him and had avoided him.

She was not sure what his view of the present situation would be, so it was with a surprise, which left no room for resentment, that she realized that he had put his arm solicitously and protectingly around her shoulder. She allowed herself to be persuaded to leave the room quietly and made no protest as he gently led her away.

Once outside, however, Carre's pretended solicitude changed to rage. He reviled the astonished girl for her intrusion upon the star.

"What's the idea, going into Paulette's room and wearing her diamonds? If you want to continue delivering your laundry here you must understand you place—and that's not in front of the star's dressing table playing with her valuables."

He motioned to Gigi who was passing. "Here, take this busy-body and get rid of her and after this keep her out of the theatre altogether."

He turned on his heel and left before the surprised girl could reply and Gigi endeavored to lead her gently to the stage door. The girl's anger welled within her and she turned viciously upon the little man. His slight frame and feeble strength were no match for the robust girl and he have up the uneaqual contest with a characteristic shrug of his shoulders. He threw up his hands in despair as he watched the angry girl follow in the direction taken by Carre. It was no affair of his; he had done the best he could and so he turned to other duties.

Marah rushed downstairs to Carre's office. He looked at her with annoyance and surprise and with grudging admiration, too, for the girl's cheeks had flushed to a pretty pink in her anger and her eyes were flashing. She was a vivid picture which Carre did not fail to appraise and appreciate.

Marah was in a desperate frame of mind, determined that the chance of coming to the theatre should not be lost to her. Before he could protest she spoke:

"Monsieur Carre, I did nothing so very terrible just now. True, I shouldn't have touched the fussy old thing's jewels, but I only tried them on to see how much better they would shine upon me than upon her." A half smile crossed Carre's lips at this little dig at the star who was growing old and whose brilliance had begun to tarnish. Marah gave him no chance to answer as she continued:

"Please do not bar me from the theatre. If you do I shall not only lose my income from the laundry, but also my chance to learn by watching the players."

Carre made no answer but remained cold and unsympathetic to her plea. In the intensity of her feeling she clutched his arm, fairly tearing at his clothes, in her frantic endeavor to change his mind. Exasperated, he roughly loosened her grip and swung in his chair around to face her:

"And if I let you continue to come and learn, as you call it, from watching the acting, what then? What do you want?"

Nothing daunted by the unexpected direct question Marah answered quickly and decisively:

"What do I want? I want my chance. I know that I can act. I know I am younger, better-looking than your scrawny Paulette with her sqeeky voice and her stiff, wooden poses. I can be a star; give me my chance"

She stood with hands outstretched in pleading, a compelling pose. Carre's momentary surprise and amusement at her description of his leading lady passed, but it left a doubt. Now that the matter had thus been brought to his attention he realized that Paulette's star was on the wane and this girl had been clever enough to see. Perhaps some of his public had seen too. It was something to consider.

Also, reasoned Carre, the girl had spirit and who knew—she might prove a find. The fickle public was always ready to welcome the rise of a new luminary, especially one of youth and charm.

It could be seen from his face that Carre was relenting. He slowly and reflectfully looked down and then indulgently gazed at the eager girl. He spoke with a meaning inflection:

"And if I give you a chance . . . ."

Marah with a cry of unbounded joy, jumped upon his desk, starting him by her unexpected prank. Seated on the edge, she leaned toward him and like a delighted child whose whim has been granted, she smilingly said softly and slowly:

"Oh, Monsieur Carre, you will give me my chance? Then I shall love you so!"

Carre, man of the world and from long experience immune to the blandishments of women, raised his eyebrows significantly. But Marah, in her happiness, did not notice the expression and contunued: "And Lucien, too, will love you so."

Carre raised his eyes in polite surprise. "And who is Lucien?" he inquired. Marah was in distress. She wanted to be loyal to Lucien, still she was determined not to lose her chance. So she temporized and did so very badly, for she hesitated before answering and was visibly embarrassed as she replied:

"Lucien?—why, er,—oh, Lucien is sort of a relative."

Carre laughed at this palpable invention. He understood perfectly and for a moment considered the unfortunate fact of Lucien's connection. Then he shrugged for he knew how to get rid of troublesome sweethearts.

"Well, we will consider Lucien later," he said pleasantly. Now stand up and let me see just what you look like."

Marah obeyed and, jumping off the desk, she assumed a pose before him. Carre regarded her deliberately from head downward. He appoved of her pretty face and likewise of her graceful figure, but when he reached her ill-shod, clumsily posed feet in his inspection, he sagged with disgust and covered his eyes to blot out the ugly sight. After a moment he looked at her and said amusedly:

"You need a rich relative."

Marah understood this hint about her cheap and ill-fitting clothes, but before she could respond he continued briskly:

"The first step to success is to wear nice clothes. And it's a necessity too, if you are to be connected with the Theatre Carre. Now this is the way you should look," and Carre, who was something of an artist, with a few deft strokes of his pencil created a picture that was the last word in smart and dashing style. "We'll see what our wardrobe lady can do, I think we have enough right here in our custumes at the theatre to rig you out."

He consulted with the wardrobe lady who responded to his ring. Earnestly and in detail he went over his sketch with her as though he was planning a costume for one of his plays. The woman nodded and motioned for Marah to follow her.

Carre had not long to wait before a new and sumptuous Marah stood before him. The change was startling; the girl who now posed for a second inspection, resembled the simple little laundress of a few moments before only in a dim and distant way. The figure that posed proudly before him, cald in rich furs and ultra-fashionable clothes, was a revelation of beauty and charm.

Carre was unprepared for so remarkable a change. With all his understanding of what extraordinary changes could be wrought with proper clothes, he had not expected to create so ravishing and beautiful a creature as the girl who now smiled upon him. He rubbed his hands with satisfaction. He reached out and took her hand in his affectionately and as he looked into her eyes, he said cajolingly"

"And hasn't our stunning little lady a kiss for her new relative?"

Marah looked at him with indecision. She had not meant to lead him on: she wanted only her chance and the clothes were a development entirely unforseen. But instinctively her hand went to the soft fur at her neck and she could not bear to risk losing this luxury. She she reached up timidly and kissed his cheek with unaffected tenderness.

Carre seemed a shade disappointed, but he said indulgently: "That is nice of you; now run along and come back in the morning and we'll see what can be done in making an actress of you."

Marah hurried home to Mme. Pigionier, eager to tell of her good fortune. Lucien flung open the door upon her knock, happiness and relief reflected upon his face to greet her safely home at last.

But immediately all joy went from his eyes, for he beheld a new, a changed Marah; a stranger. Now, before she entered, Marah threw her old clothes into the room ahead of her. It was as though she were getting rid of her old self.

The action was not lost upon Lucien, nor its signifi-cance. He watched the girl, dazed. She ws a very good imitation of a great lady as she walked with mincing steps and had held proudly high. She paused, haughtily in the center of the room, enjoying Lucien discomfor-ture and amazement. Lucien stalked toward her angrily, demanding tersely: "Where did you get those clothes

"Marah answered loftily: "Monsieur Carre gave them to me. He is going to make me an actress."

Lucien was incredulous, he could not grasp it all and mumbled doubtfully, half to himself; "You, an actress—impossible!"

Marah was hurt and drew herself up definantly as she said: "And why not, I should like to know? Why should I not be an actress?"

But Lucien disregarded her question, and voiced aloud the train of his thoughts: "You brazen, shameless girl to accept clothes from that man." His surprise and chagrin chaned suddenly to wrath. "You . . . . you . . . ." but words failed him and in the excess of his rage he struck Marah savagely across the mouth.

Marah staggered backward, staring at the man with eyes wide with horror and surprise, unable to believe her senses, finding it almost impossible to credit the fact that Lucien had committed so impossible an act as to strike her.

Lucien stared back at her, hurt and mortified, un-able himself to believe that he had done so terrible a thing as to lift his hand to this girl whom he worshipped.

Marah continued to look at him in a long moment,

wounded pride in her manner and a great hurt in her eyes. A change came over her features as her feelings revolted and all her love seemed suddenly to die from her heart. Withough a word she turned and walked toward the door.

The wretched man understood that Marah was leaving him. It was his greatest fear, his fear of losing her was now becoming a fact and he alone was the cause of it. Quivering with the pain of this awful moment which he had lived in thought so many times; faced now with the dreadful realization that what he had feared was actually happening and that he was about to lose his love forever, he pathetically called her name:

Marah turned to him sadly and speaking hardly above a whisper she said: "It is done, Lucien; our little day of sunshine and happiness is over. You have killed the love I had for you."

The frenzied man rushed to the girl and before she could reach the door, he dropped to his knees at her feet, clinging to her desperately as he said in utter abjection:

"Forgive me, Marah. I did not know what I was doing. It is all because I love you so; because I live day and night in fear of losing you." As he spoke he caressed the arm that hung listlessly at her side. He could feel that the tenseness of her figure was relaxing and seizing upon this sign of a softening in her attitude, he continued in a voice vibrating with the depth of his emotion:

"Please, Marah darling, please understand how I love you; how I worship you. Don't let anything come between us; I could not bear losing you; it would kill me."

The first shock and surprise of Lucien's unthinkable action had passed. The ice of her resentment was melting and a vision of the happy days she had spent with the abject man at her feet passed in a vivid mental picture before her eyes. She looked coubtfully down; the dear head so close to her hand was a temptation. Her hand reached hisitantlingly; it touched his hair lightly and upon the instant all her angry sorrow left her. She stroked his hair lovingly, desiring him as much as he did her. Soon she had gradually slipped to her knees beside him. So low that he could barely hear her, she breathed: "Lucien, Lucien—I only know that I love you; love you so much that I can forget all else.

Lucien arose joyfully, lifting her and clasping her to him. Locked thus in one another's arms, they failed to hear an imperative and impatient knocking at the door.

They were rudely shocked therefore when the door burst open and a gendarme briskly entered the room followed by an excited and gestulating man whom Lucien recognized with a sinking heart as the merchant from whose shop he had stolen the dress for Marah.

The merchant quickly discovered the garment where Lucien had draped it upon the chair and indignantly indicated this incriminating evidence to the gendarme. The latter, however, was more interested in the uniform which still remained upon the table just as Lucien had laid it after removing it from the hiding place in the cupboard. The gendarme pointed to the number of Lucien's regiment on the collar of the uniform; that regiment was supposed to be in Algiers. "A deserter as well as a thief," observed the officer laconically, and needed no further evidence as Lucien guiltily hung his head. Without wasting words the gendarme took out a pair of handcuffs and snapped them adroitly upon the unresisting wrists of the shame-faced Lucien.

Marah, upon the entrance of the officer, had stood uncomprehending. The dress, which until this moment had escaped her attention, brought her to a sudden realization of what the scene portended. In a flash she understood Lucien had stolen it for her. With a cry she threw her arms around him as though to protect this man she loved from all the world. With the handcuffs on her lover, Marah became frenzied in her grief. She beat with her small clutched fists upon the breast of the gendarme, but the latter brushed her aside as he would a troublesome fly that annoyed him.

Marah again threw herself upon Lucien, but he, with great tears streaming down his cheeks, was helpless to comfort her. He could not clasp her in his arms; the chill, relentless steel upon his helpless wrists was like the cold touch of death and in a hollow voice, broken by sobs, he stammered as he laid his cheek to hers: "It is not forever, Marah, sweetheart. Someday I shall be free again. If you ever stop loving me remember that I shall always love you."

Marah could not answer. Mingled love and fear choked her. She could but cling to him desperately. The gendarme decided that the parting had lasted long enough. Roughly he grasped Lucien's arm, urging him toward the door. But he misjudged the strength of the girl who clung to her lover tenaciously, fighting desperately a hopeless fight to save the man she loved; fighting against fate itself. The officer had to enlist the aid of the merchant and together they tore Lucien away. Marah in a last hopeless effort fell to her knees and clasped Lucien aound the knees. But the brute force of the two men was too much for her, and Marah fell upon her face in a paroxysm of grief as the door slammed shut with a dull sound that seemed to echo in her empty heart.

With a shudder Marah groped her way to the table. His uniform; the soldier's hat and sword. Her hand touched them reverently; with a gasp she clasped the hat over her breaking heart.

CHAPTER V

"FAME"

Marah went directly to Carre with her troubles and sobbed out the story of her grief to him. Carre was politely sympathetic, but rather amused at her sorrow and satisfied withal because the unwelcome and inconvenient sweetheart had thus been expediently removed. After listening patiently to her entreaties that he do something to help her, Carre finally brok into her pleading with: "But I cannot do anything my dear Marah. Your Lucien belongs to his country, and what France chooses to do with him is something which I or anyone else cannot possibly change."

Dumbfounded that this man, with all his influence could not help her, Marah was crushed by the thought that she would not see her sweetheart for years. She voiced the thought, and Carre confimed her fears with a careless nod of assent.

Marah considered for a moment fornlornly, and sincerely believing in her moods while they lasted, she said desperately: "Oh, but I cannot live without my Lucien."

Carre answered shortly that she was very foolish to feel that way, but the girl maintained stoutly that life no longer held anything for her.

Big tears rolled down Marah's cheeks, and Carre looked upon her as a charming child needing consolation. As though getting out a piece of candy for a sorrowing child, he delved in the drawer of his desk and drew forth the thin script of a small part in a new play. Enticingly he held it toward her as he said: "I have a small part for you. Come now, forget Lucien."

Marah glanced shrewdly at the part; this was what she wanted—her chance at last. But she remembered her grief and began to sob again.

Carre was a busy man and did not intend to waste much time with this girl. Her silly hysterics were beginning to pall upon him, too, so he tossed the manuscript back on his desk carelessly, and heartlessly offered Marah in its stead a small dagger which he used for a paper cutter. Calmly, in a businesslike tone, he said: "Here, if you cannot live without your Lucien, this is what you need. But please go outside, I dislike messes."

Carre's irony robbed all dignity from Marah's grief. It would look silly to take the dagger from him, but he was shaking it toward her impatiently as he went over some papers on his desk. She took it, holding it a moment and feeling very foolish. Her eyes strayed toward the script, and she spoke more to herself than to him: "But Lucien would want me to have my chance."

Carre nodded. "He most certainly woud," Carre answered calmly, "unless he were altogether a fool."

Marah droped the dagger and picked up the part. She glanced over the script in an April mood of smiles and tears—a tear in her eyes for her Lucien, but a smile on her lips for the part.

* * * * * *

It was the night of Marah's debut. Patiently Carre had coached her and, between his expert direction and her natural ability, she had become quite acceptable at rehearsals. But rehearsal was quite different from acting before a crowded house, such as this of tonight, and Marah was trembling as she stood in the wings with Carre at her side, waiting for her cue to enter upon the stage.

The drama was centered around a soldier's farewell. The action had progressed to the point where Jean St. Cyr, a young actor playing the rôle of the soldier, had dramatically made his farewells to his parents, and in a moment Marah was due to enter the scene. The prompter warned her, and Carre leaned over her affectionately and familiarly. He whispered: "Brace up; this is your chance; your career depends upon this moment.

Marah stiffened with an effort, taking her courage in her two hands, as it were. She walked upon the stage. The glaring lights; that great black shadow in front with its myriad of white splotches, shimmering in a sort of mist; those splotches which she knew to be the faces staring at her with eyes which seemed to burn into her very; all was confusion, and this was not at all like the stage where she had so confidently skipped through rehearsals. She tried to speak, but could not; she was confused and frightened.

Marah, numb with stage-fright, stared at St. Cyr who waited for her to speak her lines and go on with the scene. He saw that she was hopelessly out of her rôle and, to bring her back to the part, threw her a line:

"We may never see each other again."

It was a line not written into the play, words improvised by the actor in order to lead up to the confused girl and, perhaps, help her to remember her own lines. Simple words, natural to the situation but uttered at random on the spur of the moment. He was totally unprepared for the marvelous change they wrought in the girl. They were the only words that could have accomplished the miracle, for they awakened memories of Lucien, and Marah forgot in the instant where she was. St. Cry became in her imagination Lucien, and at this vision of her love Marah stood with eyes brimming with tears. A flood of memories overwhelmed her. She caught the cue from the prompter and went into a scene of love and parting that was to make her famous from that moment. She did not act the part, for she was living again her parting with Lucien. She was unconscious of self, of the stage, of the staring audience. She had projected herself back to the agonizing night of her awful parting with Lucien, and she did not act the scene but actually lived it. The audience that night proclaimed a new star.

From the small part of her first success Marah's rise was rapid. Her unexpected triumph of that first night brought with it self-assurance and, once with her feet planted firmly on the ladder leading to fame, Marah climbed the rungs with scarcely a pause. She was a natural -born actress and needed only this small spark of initial triumph to set her flaming brilliantly in the theatrical firmament of Paris.

With all her success, with the acclamations of an adoring public, with flowers and gifts lavished upon her, with wealth beyond her fondest dreams, with all these we find Marah in a corner of her luxurious dressing-room writing a letter and weeping as she writes. She brushed away the bitter tears the better ro read the words: "My beloved Lucien."

She was about to continue, when Carre entered and placed his hand over hers. Marah tried to hide what she had written, but Carre knew and only smiled. Carre believed that he knew how to cure these periodic spells of remembrance of an all but forgotten love affair, so he lifted Marah's hand, automatically making her drop the pen where it all but blotted out the name.

Marah stared at the blotted sheet, thinking how like an omen it was. Lucien almost blotted out from her life, and it was only on rare occasions, such as this, that she remembered.

She had hardly noticed that Carre slipped a jewel upon her finger. Jewels were common with her now, but the glitter of it fascinated her for a second, till her eyes again fell on the name almost blotted from the sheet on her desk. Her feelings revolted, and she tore the gem from her finger, flinging it with a sense of shame far into a corner of the room.

Carre smiled at her with a terrible wisdom. Calmly

he said: "You persist in sometimes being foolish. It is not so often now, but nevertheless it is unreasonable for you to continue at all. But if you insist, permit me," and ironically he dipped the pen in the ink and handed it to her. "There, now, write to your sweetheart in prison."

As always he had succeeded in making her feel foolish, for how useless it was, she reasoned, to write to a man so utterly shut away from the world. She impatiently tossed the pen from her, and in an effort to appear nonchalant, she walked to the corner where she had flung the ring and calmly placed it on her finger. She admired it with head held to one side, and Carre smiled with satisfaction. He was satisfied; he had no great depth of feeling for the girl and now, having accomplished his end, he carelessly kissed Marah's hand and excused himself. Left alone again, Marah was torn by cruel thoughts, and tears came to her eyes. Sobbing, she destroyed the letter she had meant to write to Lucien as she had done with many others, started, but never finished.

Through all her triumphs Marah had not forgotten the woman who had mothered her at a time when she stood in dire need. Many an hour had she stolen from her brief time of freedom in the endless round of rehersals and performances to visit Mme. Pigionier. When thoughts of Lucien threatened to undermine her path she flew to the old lady for strength, as she did now soon after her latest scene with Carre.

The little room had been kept as a shrine to her lost love. Nothing had been changed except that upon the walls were hung many wreaths of laurel, each a symbol and a trophy of her many stage successes. With each triumph and its resultant wreath Marah had hurried to her shrine, and together she and the old lady had hung them proudly on the wall.

The two were now gazing at this evidence of Marah's success, and Mme. Pigionier spoke with some awe: "Marah, my child, you must be happy with all this success," indicating the wreaths with a sweeping gesture of admiration.

Marah smiled sadly. "Happiness is in having someone to love," she said in a broken voice, and, as Mme. Pigionier looked at her sympathetically, she continued: "And, oh, someone to love me. The public adores me for a moment; then, when it leaves the theatre, forgets me."

Marah hastily brushed the tears from her eyes as Madame soothed her with motherly tenderness. "But here," she said briskly, flashing another moodlike the fickle sunshine of a showery day, "I must be going; I am already dreadfully late for rehearsal."

Meanwhile the stage was set at the theatre for rehearsal of a new play. The actors were present and waiting, everything was in readiness, but nothing could be done till the star arrived. The stage director waited patiently, with script in hand, while Carre stroke across the stage, raving in anger over the delay. "If she is one minute longer," he said hotly, "I'll . . . I'll . . ." but he saw her coming.

Marah entered serene and smiling, taking her time. She heard what Carre said, and her manner was mocking. He was embarrassed, for it would not suit his purpose to create a scene with the opening of the new play so close and announcements made. So Carre changed instantly to smiles and good nature and raised Marah's hand to kiss, like a devoted servitor. The waiting actors, who had expected a different greeting, exchanged knowing looks.

The play was a drama called "Mme. Sans Gene," with a laundry scene, and Marah momentarily thought of the coincidence of it being so like a scene from her own life.

The director called St. Cyr forward, directing him to stand with Marah at an ironing board. The stage setting was the interior of a laundry, and Marah was again impressed for a second with the similarity of the make-believe to her actual life at Mme. Pigionier's.

But Marah's thoughts were wandering, and she paid scant attention to the instructions of the director. It was a very distant and haughty greeting she gave St. Cyr as he came to her side, for the two were not on the best of terms.

Obeying the director's command, Marah picked up two laundry baskets and walked toward the ironing board. She acted with a certain amount of pantomime skill, but she was listless and her acting lacked spontaneousness.

The director was not satisfied and pointed out to her shortly where her actions were wrong. He brusquely ordered her to repeat the scene.

Marah obeyed with a certain shade of annoyance. She noticed St. Cyr's smirk of satisfaction because of her poor acting and corrections of the director, and she was nettled. When her repetition of the scene was still unsatisfactory to the director, and he commanded her to go through the business for a third time, her composure was shattered, and she dropped the baskets irritably. She said languidly: "How can you expect me to carry these heavy baskets back and forth? I am tired," and she yawned impudently.

Marah was nervous and distraught with her heartache for Lucien and not at all in the mood for rehearsal. She gathered up her parasol as though to go, whereupon St. Cyr spitefully said: "Mademoiselle used to be able to carry laundry baskets."

It was the last straw; her overwrought nerves snapped and Marah was beside herself with anger. In her blind rage she brought her parasol down upon the luckless head of her tormentor. Immediately she was contrite as in the long-ago moment wth Lucien, and, sobbing she asked St. Cyr's forgiveness. She was all compaasion and even ripped some of the chiffon from her handsome frock to bid the small wound on his head.

Carre assumed a synical, long suffering expression at these latest antics of his temeramental star and went to settle the matter.

Marah was caressing St. Cyr, murmuring tender words to him, and he, who had hated her only a moment before, was now her slave. Carre touched her signigicantly upon the shoulder. His expression was one of amusement, but from the gleam in his eyes it was apparent that he was jealous and did not intend to permit her to trifle with other men. Carre picked up her part and, placing it in her hand, said coaxingly: "It's all right now, Marah. St. Cyr has recovered and needs you no longer. Let's get going with this rehearsal."

Marah petulantly flung the script on the floor and continued to administer tenderly to the wound of the leading man who was embarrassed as Carre frowned at him. But Carre kept command of himself, and this time it was with a note of authority in his voice that he said, handing the part back to her: "Please no more of this; go on with the rehearsal."

Marah was provoked over his assumption of power over her and snapped her fingers in Carre's face. She rushed from the stage, Carre following her.

The girl flew to her dressing-room and slammed the door as though to shut out the world. She knelt at her dressing-table, from which she drew out a soldier's hat which she had kept as a souvenir of her great love. Sobbing, she pressed the hat to her heart which ached too much, and yearningly called aloud his hame: "Lucien!—Lucien!"

The door of the dressing-room burst open, and the angry face of Carre was reflected to the girl in the glass in front of her.

Marah got to her feet as Carre reached her side. She laid the cap aside and faced him defiantly, but Carre did not reproach her. Instead he took her hand and kissed the palm. Marah snatched the hand away, annoyed by his familiar caress. Excitedly she exclaimed: "I'm sick of all this, and I am through."

For the first time Carre suavity left him, and he answered with a shade of anger: "Very well, then, this ends our contract and everything."

Bowing in mock deference, he turned and walked toward the door. With a shock Marah grasped the import of his words and called: "Carre."

He turned, facing her inquiringly, waiting for her to speak. Marah was now humble and her tone was almost beseeching as she said: "I did not mean what I said, Carre. I have a headache. This hat," touching the soldier's hat with the semblance of disgust, "bah, it means nothing to me."

Carre's manner changed to indulgence, and he shrugged amusedly as he returned to Marah's side. He caught her hand again and pressed his lips to her palm, and this time Marah did not repel him, for she was frightened and realized she was in his power

* * * * * *

The high, stark, whitewashed walls of the prison reflected the blazing sun in a dazzling shimmer, so that the wretched creatures, chained together like beasts of the field, blinked and walked with stumbling steps to the waiting cells.

It was one of the few days when small privileges were granted. Visitors might call at the prison, but none ever came to see the broken, beaten man who was once the care-free singer of the happy musketeer song. Mail might be read on this day, but no letter ever came for Lucien. Magazines might be read, but none ever reached Lucien, except the cast-off copies of the luckier prisoners, such as the dirty, torn periodical that he listless glanced at now

He turned the pages slowly, calmly, hardly noticing the pictures of smart society at the races, at the beaches. Suddenly he started, trembled violently, and peered closer at a photograph on the page. It was a typical scene on the Riviera, but—the picture of the fashionable-dressed man and woman walking arm in arm, the woman smiling up into the face of her escort and talking intimately—surely it cannot be. But yes, there can be no mistake. He would know that face no matter where he saw it, for does he not see it constantly—in his tortured sleep, in his tormented days of toil, does it not smile at him every time he closes his eyes?

"Marah!"—with a terrible cry he called her name and, raving, he wrenched at his chains. Exhausted at last, he ended by falling weakly to the floor, sustained solely by the thought that months only now separated him—from revenge!

* * * * * *

Marah's pathway as she moved serenely from one success to another was a scintillating orbit in which former triumphs still flashed brilliantly to lead the girl onward to ever greater conquests.

On this night, the premiere of a drama wherein Marah essayed a rôle calling for greater powers than any previously demanded, the girl outshone every performance in the memory of even the oldest theatre-goer of Paris. If confirmation were needed of Marah's position as the foremost actress of the Paris stage it was amply given this night.

It was the end of the first act, and the Theatre Carre was the scene of a wild demonstration of public approval such as seldom, if ever before, was given to any actress. An audience, mad with enthusiasm, called incessantly for the star, who took call after call before the curtain. From the crowded gallery, where the demonstration took unbridled form, down to the boxes, where fashion and distinction were represented and where applause for the star assumed a more discreet enthusiasm, the result was the same: a delightful adoration for the young star.

As Marah took call after call, her path to the center of the stage became narrower. Flowers were banked in front, in back and on each side; from great overflowing baskets, with rare blooms to simple little bouquets, the stream of tokens came in an unbroken flow, till finally the stage would hold no more and the overflow spilled over the footlights into the orchestra pit below.

A final call and Marah returned back stage, where Carre and all the actors in the drama surged around her with enthusiatic congratulations. She was radiantly happy as Carre and St. Cyr kissed her hand by turns.

But Marah's success brought with it a train of envy and jealousy. Not all her well-wishers were sincere and among them St. Cyr, her leading man, outwardly her friend and admirer, had never lost his first distaste. It was a dislike born of the girl's great popularity, which in a way eclipsed his own fine acting, so that the public saw only Marah in every play in which the two appeared.

St. Cyr drew aside and an actress nearby whispered to him with a simper: "I don't think she is so great. You are much better." St. Cyr replied modestly but with a sneer curling his lips. The little scene had been watched by Marah, who had no doubt that the sneers were meant for her. An expression of bitterness swept across her face as she broke away from the admiring group and went toward her dressing room.

Marah was not surprised to find Rosine waiting for her. The girl greeted her mother without enthusiasm. Her attitude toward the woman was cynical, for Rosine's visits, now frequent, had not started till the girl was well on the road to success. But Rosine ignored Marah's coolness and her greeting was effusive. She rushed toward the girl and exclaimed with exaggerated affection: "My pearl, my precious pearl!" Rosine then turned to a callow young man who escorted her and introduced Marah proudly as her daughter. The youth bowed profoundly, awed and speechless in being in the presence of so great a celebrity. He considered for a moment in a blank stupid manner and then blurted: "But Rosine, how can this be? You told me you were twenty-four."

Rosine clapped her hand, too late, over her indiscreet mouth. But she had no answer and made the best of it by a matter-of-fact shrug. Rosine leaned close to Marah and poured out a lugubrious tale of her debts. Marah reached for her purse without a word, for she was used to these tales from repeated demands made upon her. She handed Rosine a generous handfull of bank notes but the latter pouted after quickly counting the notes, for the sum fell below her expectations. Marah did not wait for the protest, but with a contemptuous look emptied her purse into the covetous upturned palm. Rosine was profuse with her thanks. Now that she had obtained what she came for, she gave Marah a hasty peck upon the cheek, and taking her young man in tow, abruptly left the room.

Marah sat lost in sad reflection. Another disappointment! She sighed profoundly. Marah was now prepared for any insincerity. Lost in sad thoughts as much alone now with all her so-called friends as on her first entrance into Paris, Marah bitterly considered the farce called life.

The door opened; Marah hardly raised her head. Just another hypocrite she thought. Her eyes sought carlessly the relflection of the visitor in her mirror; strange that he should wait without speaking, with his back to the door. Curiosly she looked into the mirror again, this time to stare spellbound. This man was haggard, deathly pale, with deep lines of suffering marking his sunken cheeks, but she could not be mistaken. Lucien! With a glad cry she sprang to her feet.

But there was a terrible, desperate look in the eyes of Lucien as he reached behind him to the door and slowly, with sinister portent, turned the key.

The brooding months of heart-breaking jealousy had all but maddened him, and he came toward the girl with slow, shuffling steps, crouched like a beast stalking its prey.

Marah in her joy failed to notice his menacing attitude and rushed toward him with outstretched arms. But he met her advance with no caress, nor even an answering look of tenderness. Marah was taken aback by his strange behavior and stopped, waiting for an explanation. Slowly, so low that she could hardly hear, he hissed with a hate she could not fail to feel: "I am going to kill you!"

The girl retreated a step, thoroughly frightened.

Her shrinking goaded him on and he strang toward her. He seized the soft white throat in a strangling grip of his talonlike hands and forced the gasping girl to her knees. Lucien in his frenzy almost shrieked: "I deserted for you! I stole for you! I went to prison for you . . . ." His voice fell to a fierce, intense whisper, each syllable uttered inflaming him the more, as he continued, tightening his cruel grip on her throat: . . . "and all the time you were laughing at me; loving him!"

She tried to speak, but his hands were slowly choking her and her breath came in heaving gasps. His hands loosened at last, and he tore from her throat a beautiful necklace of diamonds. He held the jewels before her eyes as he sneered: "What good will they do you now?—you jewels!—your fame!—your beauty!"

As he uttered the word beauty he weakened perceptibly, for her beauty still held the power to sway him. There were great tears rolling down Marah's cheeks as she looked up at him. She was not afraid to die, but she was afraid that he would never know how much she loved him. In a temulous voice she said: "Those who are about to die—are permitted a last favor—are they not?

He looked at her blankly, and with deep feeling she continued: "Lucien—when I lost you there was nothing left but to die." He laughed at her madly, but with quiet intensity she went on: "I did die—I did! I killed the girl who loved you—I became the woman you see now!"

Clinging to him desperately and never once relaxing her ardent sincerity, she finished desperately: "But, oh, Lucien, bring that little girl back to life again. Take me away—anywhere—now!"

Lucien looked at her, stunned. Could it be that Marah, now kissing his hands and wetting them with her tears, was begging for his love? Slowly the fact penetrated to his numbed brain, and his heart leaped in gladness. Impulsively he lifted Marah to her feet and held her in his arms. But before he touched her lips he asked somemnly: "Do you really mean that you still belong to me?

Marah nodded and he kissed her hungrily.

Carrying out her promise to go away with him, Marah reached for her cloak. She wrapped it about her, and with a hasty look around, she took a step toward the door as Lucien silently watched her. Marah stopped short upon a loud knock. It was followed by the voice of the call boy: "Last act!"

It was the call to duty. It brought Marah suddenly to the knowledge that she had temporarily lost her senses. In a deprecatory tone she said to Lucien: "Of course I must go on with the act." She removed the cloak and Lucien looked at her strangely, not because he objected to her going on with the performance, but because he knew that the end had come.

Marah caught the look and understood it as ominous. As though to justify herself she cried: "Lucien, you can't expect me to go now; I can't disappoint my public."

Gently Lucien answered with a sad smile: "Of course you are right, Marah; but it is the last act for you and me—I am leaving you! Marah stared at him in astonishment, and he continued in a heartbroken voice: "What right have I to hold you? Can I take you back to Monmarte and poverty—or shall I live on your earnings?"

Marah knew that if she was to meet the curtain call the time remaining to her was short. Frantically she pleaded with Lucien: "I will give up everything that could come between us."

Lucien looked at her searchingly, half ready to believe, but the urgent knocking of the call boy visibly disturbed her. Lucien understood her—understood her too well, and sadly he answered: "No, Marah, you love the world too well!"

Marah, in a last desperate effort to make him understand, held Lucien a prisoner in her arms. A violent knocking at the door commenced again, and Carre's voice angrily calling for Marah could be heard. A crash of a shoulder brought heavily at the door roused Lucien, and with one last passionate kiss he tore himself from Marah's arms and disappeared through a window at the very moment Carre burst into the room.

Carre berated Marah and commanded her to go on immediately. Stunned and dazed, she obeyed, walking as one in a dream, and in that condition the raising curtain found her in the midst of a lavish stage setting showing a banquet scene.

A scene of laughter, while her heart was breaking. She spoke her lines, finishing: "No woman in the world is happier than I." A dangerous gleam of bitterness flashed into her face as she remembered that no woman actually was less happy. Still she must laugh and act her part. On the verge of collapse she continued with the lines of the play: "I have wealth and fame—and love."

Her voice broke with the word "love," and she began to lose control of herself. Dimly she remembered that it was her part to laugh. Therefore she laughed, and her laughter became wild and hysterical.

The actors on the stage and the attendants in the wings realized that Marah was not herself. They exchanged frightened, puzzled glances, and St. Cyr even made a move to steady her without dropping his part. But it was of no avail, Marah was beyond help. Suddenly her wild laughter stopped, and she glanced around her with a maniacal intensity. With a piercing shriek she cried: I can't go on!—I can't go on!"

Carre had watched the madness on the stage, waiting on the chance that Marah would get control of herself, but now cold, relentless, he gave the order that meant disgrace for Marah. "Ring down the curtain."

Slowly the curtain fell—so lightly on the stage, so heavily on the heart of an actress, for this is the final act of a career; to have the curtain rung down at the height of a scene.

Marah reached her dressing-room aided by her old friend Gigi, probably her only friend now in the theatre. She changed to her street costume and now wearily stood at the window, where she could see the great flashing electric sign of the theatre. It had been Marah's habit to stand at this window night after night, fascinated by the flashing letters: M-A-R-A-H. It had given her a sense of security and comfort, renewing her courage in times of doubt to see her name blazoned so to all the world. Now, as she looked for the comforting electric lights, she was shocked. Her name was all but blotted out, only the last letter remained and even that, as she watched, slowly flichered out light by light, till nothing but blackness met her eyes.

Erased, wiped out completely, thought Marah with a sinking heart. It was as though the final, single light, glittering for a second, to wink out into blackness, was the dying spark of her own public life.

Dismally she stared at the blank, till presently she became aware of a new letter flaming where her name had been. "S"—who?—what? Fascinated she watched, and soon she spelled out the whole name: S-T-C-Y-R. Incredulous for the moment, she still watched only dimly conscious that she was superceded. So—and she stiffened with resentment.

For a second Marah was heart-sick. Then all her courage and pride came back with a rush. It must not be the last, it could not be. Those letters of her name—they must go back into the sign. She rushed from the room.

Without knocking Marah burst into Carre's office, where he and St. Cyr were in earnest conference. The later was puffed with self-importance, since it was understood that he was to replace Marah as the box-office attraction.

Carre looked up, annoyed; St Cyr uncomfortable. Marah, determined to be brave, walked toward St. Cyr. "You," she said, "in my place?" It was a question and yet also her answer, and St. Cyr arose and bowed.

The moment was bitter, but Marah controlled herself. Brave and proud she turned to Carre and said with spirit: "This breaks my contract."

Carre, cynical and suave and dignified, got to his feet stiffly and bowed as he answered: "Yes, this breaks you contract."

Marah was shocked and frightened, but she pretended indifference as she flung her fur about her with a haughty gesture. She was magnificent in her control of herself, for she was hiding a great despair. She bade Carre a smiling farewell and graciously, but with somehwat sarcastic bow she congratulated St. Cyr. As she started to leave, St. Cyr's heart went out to her, and he called for the girl to wait. Turning to Carre, he said: "Let her stay and be my leading woman! What would become of her without me?"

St. Cyr had spoken innocently; kindly words in which he had meant to place no arrogance or conceit. Marah listened in cold silence, and her proud glance told St. Cyr that he had offended. He bowed with a muttered apology. Carre, anxious to have through with the business, left the room.

Marah, now alone with St. Cyr, had time to collect her thoughts. She realized that the young actor was truly sorry for her and had tried to do her a good turn. She laid her hand lightly on his arm as she said kindly: "St. Cyr, we have not always been friends. It was no doubt chiefly my fault and I am sorry. I think it is only to a broken heart that the spirit of kindness can enter. I understand what you tired to do tonight. I am grateful." Without giving him time to reply, she was gone. Outside the door she found Carre, waiting for her to leave. Marah threw pride to the winds and made a beseeching gesture toward him as she begged: "Can't you give me another chance, Carre?"

Carre shook his head, a trifle regretfully, yet nevertheless unyieldingly, as he answered: "There can be no second chance, for, remember, in the theatre nobody fails twice."

Marah accepted her sentence without flinching. With dragging steps she left the theatre, turning her back forever on a part of her life that already seemed to her to face into a far distant past.

Misfortune followed Marah relentlessly. In her meteoric career at the Theatre Carre she had given no thought to the future. The large sums of money that came to her slipped through her fingers like water.

She sat reading a letter from her brokers which brought the bad news that the last of her scant resources were gone in unwise speculation. Day by day her treasures were sacrificed. The splended furniture of her fine house; her superb jewels; till finally with a forced sale of her remaining personal effects Marah had but one hope. Rosine, whom she had helped so many times during the days of her prosperity, Rosine, her own mother, surely she could look to her for help.

Marah rang Rosine's door-bell with rising spirits. In the hallway she waited while the servant announced her. Marah glanced around her wistfully, confident that now she had found a home. Through the portieres she caught a glimpse of Rosine speaking to the servant. Eagerly Marah took a step towrd the man as he came to her, but his words were like a blow: "Madame in not at home."

"Not at home," repeated Marah wonderingly. "Why, I . . . ." and she started toward the drawing room. The servant made a motion to intercept her, but already Marah's pride had arrested her steps. The bitter tears came to her eyes, but she threw her head back proudly. She would not beg. Since her mother again denied her, it was the end for her as far as Rosine was concerned, and the harsh biting words, words uttered in bitterness almost on this very spot so long ago were recalled to the girl. "Pig woman," she muttered with repugnance, as she went out the door with bent head.

Beaten, her last hope so rudely shattered, Marah knew not where to turn. But yes! there was one remaining harbor. Why had she forgotten all this time? Why had she not gone there first?

On flying feet she went to the little laundry. Nothing was changed; Mme. Pigionier could be seen through the window busily engaged at her ironing board.

"Mother, I've come home," she called almost happily, but still with a poignant note in her voice. Mme. Pigionier looked up surprised, and pleased and puzzled, but Marah gave her no time to answer as she hurried up the stairs, bidding the old lady to follow.

At the door to the little room she paused a moment as she was joined there by Madame. The shrine of her many triumphs, with the laurel wreaths on the walls, symbols now of almost forgotten successes. With no word she went the rounds of the walls, collecting one by one the wreaths. With a great armful she went to the fireplace and emptied her burden.

With a wan smile she looked at Mme. Pigionier, who had watched her with uncomprehending eyes. "Now do you understand, mother?" she asked with a trembling voice. "It's all over; these little things we call successes, what are they? Forgotten like the withered leaves of last year. I am no longer Mademoiselle Marah, star of the Theatre Carre, but just plain Marah, as poor as when I came to you so long ago. Do you want me?"

There was a wistful, pleading note in the last words and it was with a cry of happiness she flew to the motherly old lady who had in answer to her question merely opened wide her arms.

The cycle of a great career has swung around to the point where it began. This day in the humble little room of her beginning Marah was setting the supper table for her lonely meal. There was the cheese, the bread; the same food of her gay little feast with Lucien long ago. She sat down wearily, breaking the bread listlessly. Memories of the gay scene so long ago overwhelmed her, and she could hardly believe that this was the very chair he sat in; there on the mantel had rested his sword and hat beside the little love clock, even now as then busily ticking the hours away.

Her glance wandered to a small table nearby, where the faded uniform with sword and hat were enshrined as the sacred tokens of her lost love. The sight of the uniform recalled her lover's brave little song:

"When I was a musketeer
A ron-ron-ron

Softly she sang the song, and its spirit brought her a little cheer. She was almost gay as the song went on,

but now she stopped singing suddenly and listened:
"When I was a musketeer . . ."

The music seemed to float to her and a dream figure of Lucien appeared before her standing in the doorway, singing. So vivid was the picture and the eerie music that Marah beat time as she listened.

Suddenly the girl jumped up from the table, clasping her hands to her head. "Can it be that I am going mad?" she muttered, and as if running away from herself she tottered to a chair where she sank down, a huddled figure of a frightened child.

Is that the door opening, or just part of this mad dream? Hopefully, fearfully, she raised her head to look. In the dim light the misty figure of Lucien entered the old debonair way, singing jauntily the brave musketeer song. It was only a phantom to torment her, she thought, and she covered her head.

But the sense of a presence in the room was too real to be downed, and again she lifted her head with frightened eyes. Only a ghost and a ghostly voice, but her name spoken in a tone she would ever remember made her sure it was he. "Lucien!"—she stared at him unbelievingly.

It was really her Lucien—an older, quieter, kindlier Lucien, who had prospered, and he said, with his arms stretched out to her: "Marah, I have come back to you."

With a happy sigh she was in his arms.

Once more the twinkling lights of Paris were a background to their love, as the two sat in the old place on the wide seat of the big bay window. Marah was clinging to his hands, and her question tripped over one another in the asking. Finally, Lucien said: "There is a ranch in South America—and a garden waiting for you."

But Marah remembered all that she had done to hurt him, and her eyes were sad as she answered softly: "But I don't deserve your love."

Very gently Lucien kissed the bright head as he answered:

"Marah dear, love is not a question of deserving; it is a question of love."

There was no more to say, and Marah rested her head contentedly on his shoulder.

THE END

The Divine Woman

Philip J. Riley's LOST FILM SERIES - Volume One
over 200 photographs and silent film titles
Plus the 1928 Novel by Marie Coolidge-Rask

www.ingramcontent.com/pod-product-compliance
Lightning Source LLC
Chambersburg PA
CBHW051840020726
47502CB00005B/1874